S0-BZG-827

Connecticut Low

Connecticut Low

By Bruce Boehm and Janet Winn

Houghton Mifflin Company Boston 1980

Library of Congress Cataloging in Publication Data

Boehm, Bruce.
Connecticut low.

SUMMARY: A 14-year-old boy who feels he has been a disappointment to his family proves himself by his heroic action during a great flood in the Connecticut River Valley.
[1. Floods—Fiction. 2. Connecticut—Fiction.
3. Fathers and sons—Fiction. 4. Friendship—Fiction]
I. Winn, Janet, joint author. II. Title.
PZ7.B635728Co [Fic] 80-16858
ISBN 0-395-29518-1

PRINTED IN THE UNITED STATES OF AMERICA
P 10 9 8 7 6 5 4 3 2 1

To Kay and Howard

The authors wish to thank the National Oceanic and Space Administration Weather Bureau at Suitland, Maryland, and the U.S. Army Corps of Engineers Hydrological Section at Weston, Massachusetts, for aid given.

1

Bud held his canoe still, bracing its delicate weight against the water's motion, to watch as small children slid down the bank, seats of their pants dark from the clay soil. In August heat, he had paddled as far as the trailer park that overlooked the river and a stream that entered the river at that point. Where the children played at creek's edge, tin cans floated, and a shopping cart lay in the mud. Bud paddled on into the stream, past the shouts, on to places where human beings did not make things ugly. When he left the river to explore streams that fed her, and he kept going until they narrowed and wound under canopies of trees, he found places quiet, secret, unspoiled, without sounds of cars or people. There he could be alone in his canoe, so silent and still that small animals came out of hiding, not knowing he was there.

With the shrieks and squeals of the sliding children still in his ears, he moved the canoe in silence, and abruptly the pointed ears of a fox appeared above the brush at the edge of the stream. Then a jay warned and the fox moved completely into sight before he left in a graceful flow, bush of red tail last. Bud had seen a deer a few years back, when he was ten. They seemed fewer now. Still there were possum, raccoons, mink, otter, still the startling pheasants and the quail.

He passed shabby houses and floated on by acres of weedy land with only trash trees, but peace, there was that. Then he saw smoke rising from a shack built just back from the stream bank. He wondered how anyone could have a fire in a structure so small. As his canoe was passing, a man stepped out of the shack.

"You, gimme a hand here."

No "please," no "how do you do"; just a "gimme." Bud was startled. Most human encounters made him uncomfortable; at least this one seemed to have got past preliminaries. He beached his canoe and went to where the man stood. Heavy rain the night before had undermined his shack. With a gesture, the man showed Bud what he wanted him to do. Their four hands thrust a heavy beam under the shack's sagging corner. Bud bent beside the man, sneaking looks at his face, deep-grooved like a relief map, at his thick, long white hair, at his lumpy hands.

"Wouldn't this be better off farther back from the water?" Bud asked.

"Nope. Wouldn't." After a while the man added, "That land back there, that's somebody else's." Then, when some more time had gone by: "This is the right place. You can hear the waterfall."

They straightened and listened together to the water.

"Thanks," the man said. "My name is Coleman. You come back sometime." And Bud was dismissed.

But he was intrigued. He paddled back to the same place two days later and found the man standing with a fishing pole in the middle of the stream. For a long time, he ignored Bud and the canoe, as if he could see nothing but his line. The pole bent into an arc and the man let line run out, then began reeling it back in. Bud sat as still as he could. The woods and the stream in the cool gray mist waited without even a bird sound. A body lifted up out of the water and splashed down in again. The old man had a quiet control; he reeled in more tightly and the fish turned and leaped but the line kept on shortening. The man was smiling, Bud saw, and whispering; it looked as if he was talking to the fish. His arm suddenly swung down with a net and the struggle was over. In the net lay a brown fish more than a foot long.

"You only need a fish pole and good sense," he said aloud, admitting Bud's presence. Sunlight was just beginning to touch the tops of trees above them and suddenly early morning birdcalls filled the light. "You get a feel about fish and animals and about the weather. What it's all for" — he cast, and the line flew out over the mist on the water — "is not television or stereo record players or those sports cars you lie down in to drive."

Bud, who dreamed of himself tearing up the roads of Connecticut in a low-slung sports car, laughed. He liked this man already.

"You don't need ree-frigerators, nor washing machines. You have those things, you've lost control of your life."

Even people in the trailer park had things like that, Bud thought. He said, softly from his canoe so that he wouldn't disturb the fish, "People need refrigerators and washing machines, to keep things cold and to get clothes clean, don't they, Mr. Coleman?"

"Coleman. Not mister. Those things only make life too easy. Easier it gets, the more pointless. Why do they want refrigerators? Because they go to the grocery stores and buy ice cream and soda pop and . . ."

"Milk?" Bud said softly.

Coleman looked annoyed, and Bud thought he shouldn't have scored a point. The man turned his back and reeled in his line. He kept his back turned for so long that the sunlight had time to reach fingers down between the trees. Bud's stomach began to grumble for breakfast and he was thinking about leaving when Coleman said, "I keep milk jugs cool in a spring. But I guess some folks don't know where the springs are. So they have to have those big heavy electric boxes to keep them tied down to one place. I'm sorry for them, that's all. It's better when you don't need anything but a fish pole and an eye for turns in the weather."

Bud kept going back to visit. Once, in November, Coleman stopped chopping wood long enough to say, "Go check my river-rat traps down to the bend there."

Bud walked away toward the bend. He had kept his huge inadequacies hidden from this man until now. Everyone else sooner or later found him out. His father had shown him, over and over, that a boy like Bud was never going to learn to do anything well. Often the exposure took the same form: "Get me a half dozen number two nails, Bud," and Bud would hunt around on the top of the workbench in the garage and be unable to find anything but a box of brads. "Can't you look?" His father would go back and get the nails himself.

What was a river-rat trap?

Where the stream angled sharply past an outcropping of steep rock, Bud stood on a stone and looked. Almost hidden in floating brown leaves and weeds, a flash of metal made him look more carefully. An animal, cat-sized, lay under the surface of the water, a dark shape.

Bud went back to Coleman. "I found it. There's an animal caught." He remembered the man had said "traps." Plural. And waited to hear about it. As usual, Bud had been stupid.

"Good," Coleman said. "Come show me which one."

Together they stood over the place. Coleman lifted the wet muskrat out of the water. He deftly opened the metal jaws of the trap and reset it in leaves and water.

"Why is it dead?" Bud asked.

"Drowned. It feels that thing clamp onto its leg and instinctively it dives. That's what it does when it's in any danger — goes under. But the wire there that the chain runs on, that's fastened to a brick down in the water. The animal carries the trap down and he can't get back up, so he drowns." Coleman waded farther, with Bud following, and he pointed. "There, see? River-rat traps go where there are trails into the rushes at the edge. That's where the traffic is. Those fellows run along their trails and pop into water when something scares them."

Bud saw another trap, at the base of a tree where a fishhead had been nailed. Coleman lifted the animal that was caught in it, dripping, sleek, long, narrow — a mink. It was alive. Coleman dropped the angry animal, swung his rifle off his shoulder and shot, hitting the mink in the head, a quick surprising sound in the early morning.

Bud's feet were cold. Wind blew the surface of the water and rattled the few leaves still hanging in the trees. The river was an unkind gray. But Coleman waded farther and Bud wanted to watch.

"Third trap is yours. Here." He handed Bud the rifle. "I hope something's in it."

His?

"See it?"

He did. He saw a dark body underwater. He looked at the animal, at the rifle, at his own feet. He felt such a wave of panic that he did not move or speak. He was waiting for the words to begin, waiting the way he waited for his father's voice. He remembered his father at the side of the town pool, three years ago, while Bud, aged ten, stood on the diving board. "You do it, Bud. No son of mine is going to refuse to try. Just get out there and dive." The words like slaps finally pushed him off the end of the board into a comedian's parody of a dive that banged his chest onto the water as if onto a solid surface.

Bud waited, but Coleman said nothing. He lifted the muskrat out of its trap and put it into Bud's hands. "Yours." The man's bushy eyebrows almost hid his eyes, but Bud could tell by their expression that it was all right. The animal lay limp and wet on Bud's bare hands. Coleman reset the trap.

"You don't need bait?"

"No, because this is a river-rat highway. They run along here every night." He pointed to a clear channel about five inches wide through the weeds just below water level. Then he pointed downstream. "There's one more trap beyond that clump of trees. You want to take a look for me?"

The words committed Bud to nothing more than finding out if the trap had caught anything. "Sure," he said. As he stepped from stone to stone, moving farther along the stream, he told himself he could try. He'd be out of sight beyond the pines. His feet in the wading boots and two pairs of thick socks felt the iciness of the day. He stamped across flat rocks and sand and wriggled his toes. He found the trap. It was empty.

When Bud told him, Coleman said, "All right. You come back again. I'll fix this one for you. Next time I'll show you how to skin and stretch 'em for sale."

Bud picked up the trap Coleman said he could have. He put it into the canoe and paddled home against the quietly flowing river. He was happy. He could learn how an animal behaves and set a trap to catch it in the act. And he would not tell anyone at home about Coleman.

2

The Taylor house was old. It crouched like a brown shingle beast at the top of a bank on the river, some dozen miles below Hartford. Paint on the windowsills was coming up like corn flakes because there were too many rooms and Bud's father was too busy working on airplanes at the airport to be painting. The family left the house by itself often. Bud's mother had places she went — he wasn't sure where — committees, church groups, places like that; Sara, Bud's sister, was often off playing with other ten-year-old girls. Closer to town, cheap new houses clustered together, all alike and with barely room for clotheslines between. They were built on filled land near the river's lip. Most of Sara's friends lived in those houses. Children lived in the trailer park, too, but Sara didn't go that far. It lay in the other direction, downriver from town, the direction Bud always took when he left the house. He came and went by water.

Bud caught the screen door before it could slam. He

could hear voices in the front room, his parents' and neighbors'. He waited in the kitchen, hoping they hadn't heard him.

"Buddy, that you?" His mother's ears were sharp.

He stood still. When they began to talk again, he climbed the stairs to his room. He kicked through dirty socks, magazines, pajamas, textbooks. From his window he could see the lawn that fell steeply down from the back of the house and lost itself in a tangle of bushes and spindly trees. Even in the dusk, he could see the opening, his path to the Connecticut River that glinted, a swift beautiful live thing out there. Above it, thin layers of clouds — stratus, his father would tell him — caught light from a rising moon.

Bud sat up late, writing out an order, from a catalog Coleman had given him, for new traps.

Ten days later, the box arrived. Bud took it, refusing to explain to his family, and opened it in the shed. He set traps where Coleman had said muskrats would be, and got up in the dark next morning to check them. In the faintest first light, he put his canoe into the river, paddled down to the stream, and then had to wait until there was enough light to see the places where grasses stood thick at the edge of the stream. In his first trap, an animal. He carried the river rat like an Oscar award, home to show his parents.

It was a mistake to put the muskrat on the kitchen table. He realized that as soon as he did it.

"Get that thing out of my kitchen," his mother said. "You put that dead thing right next to our eggs. It'll pass a disease to you. I can't stand dead things in the house."

"Buddy's got a drowned rat," Sara mocked. Sara held their cat close to the muskrat, letting the cat smell it.

His father said, "What do you want with that?"

A family is a trap, Bud thought; he took his muskrat to the shed and hid it behind bags of sand. His mother put fences all around him. Be careful not to get chilled; don't eat food that fell on the floor. Are you feeling all right? Why don't you want dinner? You should go to bed earlier. She seemed to think he was going to be sick most of the time; it was almost a prediction. His father's prediction was a different one: failure. Bud would never make anything of himself. Lazy. That word was his father's quarrel with his mother. "The kid's lazy," the father said, and the mother said, "He's just tired." Somehow Sara ran blithely out from under all of them. She played with her friends; she was always with other children. She seemed, to Bud, to live in a clear plastic bubble with the lighting of a TV stage set, where no worries, no fears, no demands could ever penetrate. She would always succeed.

The next day, when he went out on the river, Bud took the muskrat, limp in a plastic bag, to Coleman's shack.

"You'll have to skin your catch right now," Coleman said, rubbing a thumb in the fur and ignoring the flies.

"I don't know how," Bud said.

"Of course you don't. Where would you have learned that? Watch now." The man slit the muskrat skin along inside both hind legs. He freed it around the ankles and around its hairless tail. "You have to watch out not to cut into the musk sacks. We don't want that smell around here."

Bud watched. He imagined his own hands doing those same things, even felt it in the muscles of his fingers. His father often told him he was careless, awkward.

The knobby, age-spotted fingers loosened the animal's skin. "Here now, you just undress this fellow." He directed as Bud made his hands take the little body and pull the skin up over the head, leaving it inside out.

Coleman showed him how to shape a shingle into a narrow oval to push inside the pelt. He scraped away the last bits of flesh and fat. Finally, he hung up Bud's prize to dry. "Nice one," he said. "Good condition."

Bud felt different when he paddled home. He carried an enormous secret; he wasn't going to tell anyone about that pelt. He walked fast from the dock and his legs striding along under him felt good.

On a Saturday, a week later, Coleman watched while Bud did the whole job alone. At first Bud was afraid. He'd botch it. He always botched things. One evening his parents had gone out and left Bud to fix dinner for himself and Sara. He had burned a pot of beans, blackening the bottom of the pan, filling the house with the smell of scorch. They hadn't asked him to cook again. It was hung on him like a label: Bud the bean-scorcher. Sometimes now Sara made soup or muffins; not Bud.

If he started to move the knife in the wrong way, Coleman's hands steered him right, and when it was done, Bud was flooded with a hot lava of joy.

Bud paddled toward the stream to check his traps next morning. A short way from the entrance, he passed a swamp. A kingfisher dropped from a dead tree, disappeared into the water, came up with a minnow in its beak, and flew back to the tree with its rattling call. There were no other sounds. Water stood and reflected the sky in the little runways where muskrats traveled at night. Bud checked a trap he'd hidden the day before. Empty. Another he'd set under a muddy bank where the tracks had been busy. Hind foot twice the length of the front; sharp toe cuts into the mud. Muskrats had been there, but that trap was empty, too. A trap he'd put by the edge of the river was gone. Coleman had warned him not to leave traps where they could easily be found by other people. He reset the empty traps. As he walked back to his canoe, he saw prints in the mud like miniature hands with thumbs, and thought, possum. Farther along, raccoon tracks, like those of a small dog, showed up on a sandbar where the stream ran into the river. He hid a trap just underwater at the base of a tree. A piece of raw meat nailed to the side of the tree, a foot or so above the trap, might catch a mink. Then he pushed out into the stream and paddled to another hiding place for traps. There he'd won!

When he found Coleman sitting outside his cabin, he shouted, "I've got two muskrats," unable to wait until he had beached the canoe. "And a raccoon!" Pride in that, too, in the catching of the large, beautiful animal.

"I sold your last ones," Coleman said.

Sold them? The pelts that he had left drying at the shack were gone?

Coleman brought Bud a dirty envelope thickened with dollar bills. Bud felt his face go foolish with grinning. "Mine?" he said. "Thanks, thanks a lot." He had seen a Moped for sale. Now he could put a down payment on it.

Monday evening Bud hurried through dinner without speaking. "What's your rush, Bud?" His father was still cutting up the meat on his plate.

"I'd like to go into town to do some shopping," Bud said.

"Sorry. I'm not driving to town again today," Mac told him.

"I could hitch."

"You could not hitch," his mother said quickly and then looked over to Mac as if for agreement.

Bud got up and left the table.

"We are not through dinner, young man."

He came back and sat silently, watching the others eat.

Bud's mother said, "You're a stranger."

"He never talks to us," Sara said. "He doesn't like us."

"That isn't so, Sara. Your brother is just – growing away from us a bit." She made Bud feel very guilty.

He told Coleman he'd have to stay at home more. When he said that, Coleman looked up at him, his bushy eyebrows almost hiding his eyes. "Where?"

"Home. They think I don't like them or something, because I'm always gone on the river."

"You have to stay home? You have something you like to do at home? There's nothing wrong with staying home. I do it all the time. I do it because it is my choice. Is it your choice?"

Bud's mother had said to him, "You aren't leading a normal life, Buddy. You ought to be with other boys. I saw boys playing baseball at Miller's park this morning and I said to myself, Now why isn't Buddy out there?"

"Ginger's brother says Bud's weird," Sara had put in.

"I thought maybe I'd be able to sell enough of the skins to pay for a Moped," Bud told Coleman. He would not seem like a weird kid with a Moped.

"A Moped." Coleman said it flat and the word lay there between them until Bud didn't know what he wanted. He saw himself riding down West Road on a motorcycle, the engine sound giving him an authority he'd never had. He saw himself in the canoe, paddling softly under limbs of oak and beech trees that edged the creek, maneuvering easily around tumbled boards and sticks, staying the canoe to watch a flight of geese, then moving quickly on to tell Coleman what he'd seen. You had to choose; you couldn't be both people. The boys in his class at school all clustered around the first Moped and its owner last fall. The same boy owned a snowmobile, too. Power. He could cover so much ground so fast. He could make a noise huge enough to make everyone on the street turn and look. Bud knew what Coleman thought of motorcycles and snowmobiles. That was obvious.

"They think there's something wrong with me," he explained to Coleman. "I'm not regular. I guess they think I'll turn out to be some sort of mess."

"What's that – some sort of mess?" Coleman asked him softly.

A dead raccoon lay at their feet; the old man sat silently beside Bud on the long bench, watching a pair of mallards work their way up the creek, dipping into the water to feed, lifting their heads again, sunlight catching the shimmer of gold in green feathers. The ducks muttered to each other as they drifted on the water. Then a jay screeched some warning and the mallards lifted off the water and away. When they were gone, Coleman said, "Come in here," inviting Bud into his cabin for the first time, as if watching the ducks together had made some difference between them. He showed Bud a sketch of ducks he'd made and tacked to the wall. There were watercolors, ink sketches, charcoal sketches, crayon drawings, all of animals and birds, making a patchwork quilt of the cabin walls.

An army cot, wood stove, shelves of pots and pans and cups and glasses and worn books; a small cupboard, two chairs at an enameled kitchen table; there was nothing else. Bud would have liked to live there forever. Once, in December, Bud spent all day in Coleman's cabin. It was warm in there, even when there was ice on the stream, and smoky from the fire. The room was filled with smells — smell of pelts, smell of pipe tobacco, a raspy sharp pipe tobacco, smell of stew. Coleman was cooking a muskrat Bud had trapped. He cut up onions and turnips and carrots, sliding them off his cutting board into the pot. "There. I let those talk to each other. You inviting me to dinner tonight?"

Bud was confused at first. The image of himself leading Coleman through the front door of the Taylor house, in his shapeless, no-color sagging pants and his shirt with stains at war with a disappearing plaid, and introducing this man to his mother and father, seemed impossible.

"It's your river rat," Coleman said, looking up at Bud from under his eyebrows. "So it's your dinner."

"Yes, sir." He hesitated. His mother would panic if Bud weren't home, and on time, for dinner. She cried when she was frightened, and she was afraid so often.

And his father, who never seemed to fear anything, would be outraged. "I'll have to ask my folks if I can stay."

The old man's look was skeptical, questioning. What did those eyebrows of his say? "You look to me as tall as a man. You can trap your own dinner," he said. "But they must like to have you there for meals."

Bud paddled the long way, in places breaking ice, with a wind like a razor blade at his neck and ears, back home, and they told him, No, under no circumstances was he staying out for dinner, especially when he couldn't – or wouldn't – be clear about where or with whom.

Bud watched his mother's face when she was saying No. Tension pulled her mouth taut.

He had not said anything about Coleman. He only told them he wanted to eat out.

"Where?" his father asked.

Where? "By myself. In my boat."

"In this weather?" his father said.

"You'll get wet. You'll take cold," his mother said. "You might tip over your canoe in the dark."

They knew Bud could never do anything except clumsily. Sara and her friends, two girls, giggled on the couch. Friendship was something else Bud fumbled. Sara had friends, gaggles of them, but Bud could not manage the business of being a boy that other boys wanted to be around. Something stiffened in his manner; his words came out awkwardly; he shielded himself with the conviction that the boys in his class were boring. How could they care so much about so little? They stayed in clusters and left him out. Sara and her friends were just such a cluster, laughing at him. Bud went to his room and slammed the door. Coleman ate the muskrat stew alone, Bud supposed.

3

"How about taking a trip with me, Bud?" Mac Taylor stood in the doorway of Bud's bedroom. "You haven't been doing anything useful with your time."

Downstairs, piano notes chased up a scale.

It had been a hard winter on the river; too much ice for the canoe and too much snow for hiking along the river's edge. Now that spring was coming, Bud could be out there, trapping, soon. He kept his back to the doorway, pretending to do homework. But he knew without looking exactly how his father stood, leaning with one shoulder against the frame of the door, blocking the way out. A posture that made Bud feel small and clumsy. The view out the window was what he wanted to look at, anyhow. Moonlight was beginning to make deeply dark places in the yard, changing it from some place familiar to a place full of possibilities.

"Bud."

"Yeah, Dad?"

"You should come on this flight with me." When Mac Taylor said "you should" that meant "you have to."

Bud nodded.

"You've been at loose ends; it's time you shape up. I have to fly to Detroit to pick up engine parts. You come along; it'll give you something to do with a couple of days of your spring vacation."

Bud had so much to do with his vacation days; the river lay out there beyond the moonlit yard, curling smoothly as if someone were pulling a piece of silk. Bud had been on a few of those plane trips with his father. Bumpy air scared him and made him sick.

"Bud?"

"Yeah, Dad, when are you going?"

"Thursday."

That was it. At least, when the air was smooth, Bud could lose himself in dreams up in the sky.

During the next days, Bud watched as ice along the river edge and in the creeks began to thaw. He liked seeing thick chunks break away and move with the stream. Two days of rain could not keep him indoors. He slopped through the wet grass and puddles, glad to be out.

Then he woke on a morning of sunlight that glittered in raindrops that still hung in the trees. The sky was a bowl of light at dawn. The trees stood still, in wait for leaf buds to swell.

What day was it? He rolled over on the bed. Thursday. Detroit in the plane. He'd get sick and his father would be contemptuous. How could the son of a pilot get airsick?

Downstairs, plates clattered. The radio came on. Bud found himself listening when the weather report began. Across the mountains through Pennsylvania, it was clear with winds from the west. In Ohio the winds backed around more from the southwest, shifting to south with increasing clouds.

Bud went down to breakfast. His father was on the phone. He hung up and said, "You don't look ready for a flight." Bud buttoned his shirt.

"There's a low pressure storm area moving into Iowa from the west and it will be close to Chicago early tomorrow morning. Another storm is developing in the south Atlantic and that one will move up the coast. Weather in Pennsylvania will be messy coming back tomorrow, ahead of the storm. From what they tell me —" he indicated the phone — "we should come back to Connecticut through Canada and Buffalo, to stay north of trouble."

Bud sat down and looked at the platter of scrambled eggs. Sara was picking pieces of bacon from the edges of the plate.

"Stop chewing your lip, Bud," his mother said. "Would you rather have shredded wheat?"

He would rather have a day on the river.

Wind scudded leaves along the surface of the airport

and bent the grass where Mac Taylor's small plane was parked. Bud stood watching his father walk around the flimsy craft, checking, moving ailerons and elevators, inspecting, pulling the propeller through a turn. Apparently satisfied, Mac tossed a suitcase onto the seat in back and they both climbed in front. Seatbelt fasteners clicked. Bud, the back of his neck tight, thought, I could still get out. I could undo the seatbelt and just get out. There is still time.

His father pressed the starter button.

"Taxi straight ahead and hold at active runway thirty; wind two six zero at six altimeter zero zero four," the radio in the cockpit said.

The plane waited at the end of a runway. Mac ran the motor up to full power. "Six-six-A ready to take-off," he said, and the radio came back, "Six-six-A cleared for take-off." The runway began to flow under the plane, then it was rushing under, finally it sank away. The plane had done what Bud could never believe, even while he was experiencing it: they had pushed themselves off the earth and were moving in the air.

Bud stopped digging his fingernails into his palms and let himself breathe. Down below, houses and streets were model-size, part of a make-believe world, where it seemed you could reach down and rearrange a barn here, a fence there, pick up a railroad track and put it down farther back from the river. The world below did not vanish as it did from the window of a jet. In his father's plane, Bud could become engrossed in the scene flowing under him. He had a fantasy of flying, planeless, with his arms outstretched.

But his father jolted him back into the cockpit. "Farmington River's really high. Last week's warm weather and the rain must have thawed a lot of snow."

Bud looked back along the meandering river to where it met the Connecticut north of the city. All through New England, rivers were probably running full now. In back of their own house, the river rose higher on the dock posts than usual. Could it turn Coleman's spit of land into an island? Coleman had told Bud he didn't know how to swim.

"We should be in Detroit in five hours – maybe less."

"Five?" Bud said. "Why so long?"

"A high." That was Mac's style – cryptic – except when he delivered a full-scale lecture.

Bud said, "A what?"

"High pressure area. Yesterday it was over Wisconsin. Today it's over West Virginia. Since wind is circling a high in a clockwise direction, it blows toward the west at the lower part of the circle and toward the east at the northern part of the circle. We'll be flying along the top of the high, with our nose right into the wind."

"Does that slow us up so much?"

"Of course." Stupid question. "You mind a little bouncing?"

Mind? He loathed it. "No," Bud said.

"Because you're going to get some. Warm air down

there coming up here. Making those fluffs of cloud at the top of each column."

Bud imagined transparent elevator shafts in the apparently benign sky, each shaft topped by a cottony cloud. The plane began to fly through the columns; it bounced, rose and fell; Bud tightened with each lift.

"Didn't the man at the airport say there's bad weather coming?" Bud asked.

"Oh, well, you never know whether it will amount to anything. Rains and flooding aren't unusual this time of year."

Bud pulled into himself, and the oily feeling in belly and throat was there as he searched the sky for clouds. Suppose they had to fly through a storm. Suppose a storm came and flooded the river at home. That must not happen this year. Nothing must interrupt the turning of the year to spring in his and Coleman's river world.

Another bounce. Bud wondered, what happens to a light plane in rough weather? This bumpy air would be nothing compared to a tossing, roaring northeaster wind.

Later the plane stopped bouncing and became still, as if it were hanging motionless in the air. At twice the speed of their car on the main highway, the plane seemed stationary. A cloud sailed past below them. They were above the elevator shafts now; that was why the bumping had stopped.

"When would we see signs of a storm?" Bud asked.

"It could cloud up as we fly over Ohio."

"What about tomorrow?"

So lightly, so casually, Mac said, "If the low from the west comes in, and the other one moves on up the Atlantic coast, they might both chase us home."

Bud looked over at his father and did not dare to tell him how terrible that sounded.

"I expect drizzle or light rain, maybe some snow with it, will be around by morning," Mac said. "The parts I want at Detroit will be waiting for us at the airport. We'll load the plane when we get in and aim to get an early start home, because during the night the wind is going to swing all the way around and be coming from the east."

"Head winds going back!" Bud was cursing himself for having come on this miserable trip.

"Sure. No sweat. That's the luck of light plane flying. Take it as it comes. Don't go turning pale over it." Mac turned on the radio.

Weather chatter came through the speaker. "Des Moines, Iowa, thunderstorm, heavy rain, wind gusty, visibility one half mile. Low pressure center moving east at twenty-five miles an hour."

Bud's stomach reacted with a twinge. "I hope the storm doesn't get to Detroit sooner than you figure."

The upper Delaware River slid past below them; it was swollen. The small plane flew through clear air with the world visible for forty miles in every direction. They passed above Scranton.

"There's a lot of snow on the ground ahead," Bud said. "Up that high there hasn't been much melting."

From Williamsport, they followed close to the Susquehanna River for sixty miles. Another high river.

Bud began to daydream, picturing his own canoe on every one of these rivers. As the plane's motor hummed quietly and he seemed to be motionless in the air, he imagined passing silently through quiet stretches of a river where there were no houses or towns. There the river would be his own, its secrets his to discover: a hidden inlet, a small island, streams too shallow for any boat but his, places where he could fish and trap and find wonderful animals to bring back to Coleman.

"*Special weather advisory.*"

Bud jolted awake. He'd been sleeping for an hour. The radio voice said, "Severe storm warning."

Bud sat up and listened.

"Storm warning from North Carolina through New England. Storm center to pass Chesapeake Bay area . . ."

"Where are we?" Bud asked.

"Close to Ohio."

"He said severe storm, didn't he?"

Mac looked over at Bud as if daring him to be afraid. "We'll leave Detroit early. You'll have to get yourself out of that motel bed by six-thirty in the morning. With the storm center reaching Virginia by morning, we'll be right ahead of it."

Bud could not muster the calm his father wanted. He

knew he would be awake long before six in the morning.

66A passed the end of the Detroit City Airport. Mac reduced power, turned into the traffic pattern on base leg, and, swinging into final approach for runway 21, was given clearance to land. Close to the runway, one hundred feet above the ground, he took all power off the engine and put on full flaps. Bud's stomach was boiling. More than any other part of flying, he hated landings. The plane rushed along a few feet above the runway, losing speed, settling down, and then made contact with the earth.

Legs shaking, Bud got out of the plane. He looked up. Over Ohio, he had seen thin, high, torn strips of clouds. Here the clouds were lower, forming a continuous thin layer through which the light of the setting sun shone weakly.

He helped his father load packages of parts into the plane. Locked, fueled, the frail yellow bird was left ready for early morning take-off. Bud gladly walked away from it.

4 ✣ Bud relished the plushy comfort of the carpeted room; he liked being able to watch color TV from a bed. The television camera was following a trim jacket-and-tie man through corridors of a meteorological center. Teletype machines rattled out word of weather conditions to all corners of the country; computer wheels rotated; radio messages came in; people bent over drawing boards or sat at computer consoles. A woman showed a film, a speeded-up series of pictures taken from satellites, showing the clouds around a storm center, turning and swirling in a counterclockwise direction while the whole formation moved northeast across the United States.

As Bud was dozing off, a man spoke, Adam's apple moving his necktie knot, "a brain receiving and sorting . . . every six hours," and the screen showed a national weather map with its waving lines, made up of all the information coming into the meteorological center. A brain. Bud fell asleep thinking about a brain, a huge brain controlling, processing, bringing in data so that men could do battle with swirling, seething storm centers.

By six in the morning, Bud and Mac were in a diner. Mac ate three fried eggs and then, because Bud could not get down the pancakes he'd ordered, Mac ate those, too. Bud, by daylight, had lost his faith in a carpeted, perfectly instrumented and controlled world that would not let a mere storm harm a citizen. His father said, around a mouthful, "Flood alert on, from Virginia all the way up the coast."

Bud wondered if Coleman had a radio. "Do they send that news to all the radio stations?"

"Of course. Planes and ships have to get it. It goes out to radio stations everywhere. People need to know."

Bud nodded. But would they know in time?

Mac Taylor took his plane east on a course nicking over Canada along the north shore of Lake Erie, then Buffalo, keeping away from the storm center that lay to the south. He flew on instruments in light rain and snow, as they left Detroit. The plane's radio brought in reports of rapidly worsening conditions in Michigan and Pennsylvania.

Bud hated the flying in rain and clouds. He was in a trap made of blank gray walls. Nothing ahead but the rain streaking back across the windshield. What might come at them out of that cloud they were in? Were they headed toward home at all? Were they turning? Climbing? Diving straight down? What about other planes flying in this same cloud? Someone somewhere was supposed to be watching this and any other planes in the area on radar, to keep them separated, to warn if one strayed off its course. Instruments and someone watching radar. He did not believe it, any more than he really believed an object as large and heavy as a plane could move off the ground and fly.

"Let's get out of here," he said. "Get us home ahead of those storms." He heard the fear in his own voice.

Mac gave him a look, and Bud was ashamed, but no less afraid. The air was smooth. His stomach shouldn't be bothering him. But just the thought of those storms was enough to give his belly pains.

Mac got the signal that the plane was passing over London, Ontario, and he reported to Air Traffic Control. They gave him information about another plane about to pass him.

Shortly before they reached Buffalo, the radio was on, giving a weather broadcast, and a special advisory came in: "Severe storm and flood warning from Virginia through New England. Storm center in North Carolina. Precipitation extending through Pennsylvania, New York, and southern New England by late afternoon."

Bud could not make himself relax. His hands ached from clenching. At least they were no longer inside of a cloud. The layer of thickness had lifted and now was above them. The lake shore and Buffalo were visible up ahead through a mist. The rain had become a drizzle. Still his hands knotted together. He could not shake the feeling of being pursued. The storms would close in, coming closer, racing the plane, moving faster than it could fly, pursuing until it was caught. To be home — now! Did Coleman know what was happening? He was good at reading signs of weather change, but would he know how bad this was going to be? Would he leave his cabin? Where could he go?

Passing Buffalo, Mac altered course to go home over Binghamton and Poughkeepsie. Wind blew from the northeast, not quite a head wind and not as strong as when they left Detroit. This helped their ground speed. As they left the lake behind, the clouds were higher above them. Then, three quarters of an hour out of Buffalo, the clouds seemed to be coming down again. Bud could just make out the Finger Lakes. They crossed Watkins Glen at the southern tip of Lake Seneca. Another weather broadcast reported rain at Williamsport, Scranton, and Newark, New Jersey. The storm and flood warnings were repeated. Rain to spread through New York, Massachusetts, and Connecticut.

"In Connecticut? It's raining now?"

"Not yet. But it will. The river is already high enough, damn it; we're going to get just the storm we don't want."

"Enough to flood beyond the way it goes over its banks every spring?"

"Maybe. This is two storms at once. The one moving up the coast pulls more and more wet air in from the ocean. The other one, following us in from the west, grabs moisture from the Great Lakes. Those two storms could make one huge low all over eastern New York and Pennsylvania and New Jersey and most certainly over Connecticut. Rain will fall on our valley and keep on falling, and then it will fall over the tributaries that come into the Connecticut River from the Green Mountains and the White Mountains. Rivers all the way up to Canada will be loaded."

Mac Taylor was leaning back, relaxed, enjoying himself. He talked about the Atlantic Ocean and the Great Lakes and a whole winter's snows from all the New England mountains, all falling at once on his piece of the Connecticut River, and he looked as if he liked the excitement of it. Mac's face was bony and always tanned, even in March when most people were pale. He'd get a look of keen pleasure when he was doing something that took care and close attention, like piloting a plane into an airport with a crosswind or taking apart the motor of their car. Bud wondered how he could possibly look that way even now.

"When would floods hit our part of the river?"

"Day after tomorrow. We'll have to assume the worst and get ready for it."

What did Coleman do to get ready for a flood? Bud wondered. He must know the signs, must have somewhere to go. He'd spent years hunting and fishing and trapping along the river, hadn't he? He must have understood the risks when he built his cabin so close to the water. Coleman had told Bud he'd never learned to swim. But it wouldn't come to swimming; it couldn't come to swimming. Coleman would pack up his pictures and pots and pans and skins, and go to higher ground.

Clouds blew past the plane window. Then 66A was inside a cloud, and Mac was flying the plane on instruments again. Bud felt the pressure of those converging lows in his stomach. He wanted the plane safely back on the ground, and quickly, before the winds and rains came. He willed it home. Hurry.

"Maybe we'll get lucky. Maybe we'll have two days to get ready for this thing," his father was saying. "We'll find out where houses are likely to be flooded and see what can be done. Sandbag barriers. Bags will have to be filled." Mac Taylor had filled sandbags before, during a lifetime on the Connecticut.

Bud thought of the river as he had left it. The water had been high, full of ice, but beautiful. "What about the boat?" he asked. "Do I have to drag it up to the house?"

"No. It could be useful. Somebody will make a list of boats available. Moor it where it can't get away in high water. Did you get your canoe up into the shed? When we are home, I'm going to have to find out if sandbagging crews have been organized. There will be plenty to do out at the airport, too." Mac sounded as if he relished the challenge. Bud cringed.

A whirlpool of damp air from the east was moving in through the Catskill Mountains. The air, being pushed up by rising ground, was cooled and condensed into low clouds. The gray of the skies and the gray of the earth below, winter-stripped of leaves, bare of snow blankets except in high places, made the world a bleak place.

Traffic Control told Mac to bring 66A down to 5500 feet. An hour later, over Kingston, he was told to descend farther to 3000. They still flew through cold grayness. Another half hour brought them into the final approach at Brainard Airport. Solid earth lifted to meet them. Solid, wet earth, for a drizzle had started.

"I'll be making another trip to Detroit in three weeks. Want to come along?"

Bud didn't answer. With his feet on the ground, he felt safe. But he had held himself so tightly for so long that muscles in his neck and back ached. At least he hadn't been sick. He had no intention of flying to Detroit, not in three weeks, not ever. One thing had happened to him on this trip, he thought. He had reached a point where he would tell his father no. Next time. "Dad, didn't we leave the car windows open?" he said, avoiding reply to the invitation.

5 Bud set his suitcase on the hall floor and headed out through the kitchen. His mother's voice was pitched high with worry. Why had they flown in bad weather? Now that Bud and Mac were safely home, her fear was turning to anger.

Bud went into the shed. He touched his canoe; it would have to wait a little longer before he could paddle down to Coleman's stream. He knotted a long hawser onto the rowboat. It had an outboard motor; Bud felt no love for the thing. Where it went, birds and animals fled. But his father had said it could be useful during a flood. When the storm was over, Bud would take out the canoe; he would try again for mink, he promised himself. But for now, he'd set just one trap, right here at the edge of the river.

In the quiet of rain falling on the ground around him he climbed the hill back to the house. Raccoons were going to be short of food, he thought; they'll be hungry and on the prowl, with the river so high. He could make a set on the bank below the house where a group of trees stood well above the river. His own muddy footprints trailed him across the kitchen linoleum as he found a small piece of raw beef in the refrigerator and went out again. The meat he fastened on a tree. He set a trap below, covering it with leaves.

During that night, Bud woke. He lay wondering what had broken into his dreams. Wind made bare branches rattle and rain splashed against the window, running thick and loud down the rainspouts. Then he heard the sound that had waked him: a dog howled. It was down by the river. Bud rolled over and tried to sleep and the dog went on howling. Bud told himself he knew why and he ought to get up. That dog was caught in the trap he'd set for raccoon. Get up in the cold, dress, and go out in the rain. Coleman had told him it wasn't easy to release a dog from a trap. The dog could be hurt and frightened and very likely to bite. Bud pushed back the blankets and sat up. Curtains of rain blew past the window. The dog howled again, his voice more stricken and plaintive now. Bud stood up. Then he heard his father's feet on the stairs. The back light came on and Bud could see him going through the rain toward the river. Bud got under the covers. A failure again; dumb; guilty.

When he stood at his window in the morning, rain blew in. The windowsill was puddled; the rug beside the window squelched wetly under Bud's feet. Gusts of wind flipped the curtain. The river ran dark brown and sullen. Over it a half dozen black ducks flew low, moving restlessly upriver in search of a marsh sheltered from wind. With a surge of fear, Bud realized the water was visibly higher. The level of the water was very close to the tops of the river's banks.

What if those two storms did meet here?

Mac Taylor leaned his elbows over the table, his spoonful of corn flakes dribbling milk on the morning paper. "Your damned trap caught an animal last night," he said. "Didn't you hear the howls?"

Sara reached across the table for suger, a thin ten-year-old arm. "It's mean," she said. "You don't even care how much you hurt them."

"It was a dog and it tried to bite Mac," Bud's mother said. "That's a very dangerous situation."

"The poor dog was in pain," Sara said.

"Yes, I suppose," her mother granted.

"Bud doesn't even think of that, I suppose," Sara said, small unconscious mimic of her mother.

Bud could only sit down and fill a bowl with cereal. That gave him somewhere to look. He had thought about the animals in traps; he had thought about them a lot. At first the thinking about it had made him feel very lonely. There had been times when he would have liked to come home and talk about it with his family, but he had never believed they would let him go on trapping if they knew he was questioning it. Coleman knew a lot about how to trap animals with the least cruelty; Bud had leaned on that.

"It does seem thoughtless — brutal." Bud's mother always spoke a little tentatively, as though willing to accept any disagreement.

"It doesn't have to be cruel," Bud said. "I am sorry about the dog. What happened to it?"

"I let it loose. Paw was pretty bloody. He just limped away. He didn't really try to bite me; your mother exaggerates. I just said it was a possibility."

Coleman would not have let the dog limp away. Coleman did have feelings for animals. Hadn't he made a pet of a baby squirrel that had fallen out of a nest? He told Bud the squirrel had slept in Coleman's shoe at night. And a fox; Coleman had had a pet fox. "You can do that if you start when they're young enough. That's the dog in them. They can care — for a while, anyways. He left me one day." Coleman would have done something to help heal the dog's paw. When he caught a wild animal in a trap, and it was still alive, Coleman killed it quickly. He would never leave a hurt animal to take care of itself.

He'd said, one morning when Bud found him feeding seeds to a chipmunk, "People and animals, they've always lived together — and eaten each other. It's the nature of things. I don't happen to like the taste of chipmunk," and he'd had a really gentle look, with his hand down on the ground, palm up and full of seeds for the small animal that sat by his fingers.

"Don't you ever put a trap out on this property again," Mac said. "That's that. Now —" and he shook out the morning newspaper — "take a look at that."

There was a story from Michigan with a picture taken at the west end of Lake Erie. The paper headlined in red caps, DISASTROUS FLOODING. In a photograph, a wave was rolling up to the canopied entrance of a luxury apartment building.

"I knew it," Mac said. "And there've been heavy rains and rising rivers in Virginia, Maryland, eastern Pennsylvania. Look at this." He turned to the weather map. "We're in for two days of this and another day of downpour in the northern parts of our river basin before we're through."

Bud thought of the heavy brown water rolling between the river's banks already. "Flood?" he asked. "Here?"

"Oh, it does that every spring," Sara said.

"I think," Mac said, standing up, making it into a speech, "the river will go over its banks and then over all the old flood records."

Bud's mother gasped.

Bud could remember times in the past when the river was roiled and muddy, and it tumbled across the tobacco fields and washed over the VFW picnic grounds. Basements of houses in low places filled with water, sometimes even a few first floors. But the damage was only muddy floors. Floods of real seriousness had taken place long ago, before Bud was born.

"It's because there are two storms coming together and there's so much snow that will melt into it in addition," Mac said. Bud wondered whether his father was worried — or perhaps a little pleased. Bud thought of Coleman's tiny hut.

"Dad, we have to do something," he said. "We've got to stop it."

"*Stop* it?" Mac laughed at him. "Stop a flood!"

But it had to be stopped. You couldn't just stand back and let it happen, let Coleman's hut be washed away. "Isn't there something to do?" He thought of the trailers close to the river's edge. He thought of the houses built recently on fill. Weren't those people going to be in danger? Bud stood, too, facing his father, hating him for having laughed. "*I*'m going to do something."

"Okay, okay. Sit down. You don't put your hand out and order a storm to halt. Finish your breakfast. There are some ways we can be useful. You see to our boat. No. Not now. Finish eating. It won't float away yet. Double-moor it with a long hawser up to higher ground, so it won't break loose, and so we can reach it if it's needed. See that the gas tank is filled. Then maybe we can help somewhere with sandbags. If only this town were organized. Old-timers have a way of sitting back and saying, 'We've lived through floods; don't tell us.'

And newcomers don't know a thing. Civil Defense sends out warnings and nobody listens."

Bud's mother took away the empty cereal bowls. Bud went outside on the porch, moody and restless. It had not bothered him to see those small animals die. His mother and Sara said things that made him feel he ought to mind, as if there were some lack in him. He'd watched the way Sara played with cats. She put dresses on old Oedipus, and ribbons, and put him in her doll carriage. The cat's tail switched and his ears lay back and he glared in outrage. Bud's mother could hold the cat in her lap, stroking his fur, talking to him, and then leave him alone in the house for three days while the family went away. Sometimes Bud looked at the cat and the cat looked at Bud, and Bud wondered what it thought, and then the cat's looking at him made him uncomfortable.

The animals that lived by the streams and in the woods were far more beautiful, to Bud, than cats and dogs. Somehow they had greater dignity. Coleman said Indians had hunted these same animals in the same places, and often in the same ways. Other animals hunted them, too. For that matter, Sara's cat sometimes left four squirrel paws and nothing else from a hunting trip. "Man is part of nature," Coleman said. "And that airport where your father works, where they're filling in swamp to make a new runway, that does more harm to small animals than you or I could do in twenty years. I have no use for people who sentimentalize over the poor trapped animals and then tie up a dog. You ever listen all night to a tied-up dog?"

Inside the house, Bud could hear people going up and down the stairs, clattering pans in the kitchen, moving boxes or something else heavy. He went indoors to find out what was going on.

"If people are going to be flooded out of their homes," Bud's mother said, "I have to find out how many extra blankets we have. I could make sandwiches and coffee. We have a big house. People may be brought here."

Bud was impressed. When the need was real, suddenly she was serene, collected, matter-of-fact; her hair in a braid down her back, wearing her old bathrobe with the frayed sleeves, she was planning rescue operations. She even forgot to scold Bud for wearing sneakers out into the rain, instead of boots.

As he walked down the yard, he could feel the weight of the wind. It stopped him for a moment, like a huge hand placed on his chest. This wasn't play. There was something — he wet his lips and knew he was afraid. A gust slapped the hood of his rain shirt against his cheek.

The river was high on the piers of the dock and although the Taylors' bit of shore was on a sheltered curve, where the water was usually quiet enough for a canoe, today dark water rushed over the edge of the dock at high speed. He pulled on the rope of the boat and felt the river drag against him.

Already the water was higher than it had climbed during last spring's flood. Moving fast, swirling around the dock in thick brown coils, it tugged at the boat.

Today no canoe could be handled in this water. But his father's dinghy with its outboard would take Bud down to the place where the creek Coleman lived on entered the river. Once Bud was into the creek, he'd have no trouble at all. He started the motor.

"What do you think you are doing?" Mac Taylor stood at the back door, shouting. "Tie that boat up."

Bud got out and carried the hawser up to high ground. He ran it around an oak tree and knotted it as tight as the knot inside himself. Then he walked toward the house without looking up. He knew his father still stood there.

"That was absolutely against orders."

Bud looked at the mud on the toes of his sneakers.

"Irresponsible, undisciplined. You're childish, Bud, just childish . . ." The voice rained down on him. Mac always had trouble stopping once he started these tirades.

Bud tried to pass his father's feet and get indoors, but a hand clamped on his arm stopped him. "You think that river out there is a wading pool, you can just go out anytime you want to and play in it. Well, you can't. And not in my boat. That boat is going to be needed by adults. You probably didn't tie it tightly enough for this water."

The sight of Mac's back, as he walked downhill to check the hawser, stiff with disgust and anger, was worse than the words had been. Bud went up to his bedroom.

He knew that Mac Taylor believed there is a right way to do things, and a definition of a good person, and that it is necessary to struggle against weaknesses in oneself in order to be a good person who does things the right way.

The day that Bud skinned his first possum, behind Coleman's cabin, fighting off circling flies, working very slowly, looking up sometimes to see, by Coleman's face, that he was doing it right, Bud told Coleman about his father, or rather about himself and his failures in his father's eyes. It all just came out, there in the sunlight with the sound of water on stones nearby and the work in his hands to keep him from being self-conscious while he talked.

After a while, Coleman asked him, "You think he's right, and that's that?"

"Yeah," Bud said. "Well, he sure does a lot that helps other people."

"What? What does he do?"

"He repairs airplanes. He sells parts for planes."

Coleman was quiet, scraping a pelt. Bud thought the subject was dropped. Then Coleman said, "Okay. What he does is he helps people. And what I do, it doesn't help anybody. So that means I haven't earned the right to take up space in the world?"

"Oh, no!" Bud protested. He was embarrassed because Coleman had expressed very baldly exactly what Mac Taylor probably believed. Bud did not want Coleman to feel inferior in the way that he, Bud, felt inferior. That would be all wrong. He felt he shouldn't have talked about his father at all if it was going to have such a result.

Coleman said, "There are different ways to see. If you are taught to see in one way, it will be very hard to see in any other way. Like all of us having special lenses in our glasses. The people in this place have lenses that see my life as shiftless, wrong. For them, what is real, really there so that you can put a hand on it, is your father's sort of life. Not mine. But that isn't the only possible way to see."

Bud watched Coleman's face, shadows and sunshine moving across it as a breeze shifted the branches of a tree above them.

"For me, those highways out there aren't real things. I've used them, a bit, but the way other people take to the woods for a vacation. You know the woods aren't real things to them." He was silent and Bud scraped at the hide of the possum, thinking.

"What makes somebody feel good, that's important, isn't it?" Coleman said.

Bud nodded.

"What does your father do just for a good feeling?"

The question baffled Bud. Coleman was a stranger — a secret in his life. Nobody knew that Bud came here and talked to a friend. These were hours stolen, like daydreaming. He came here and sometimes he told Coleman about his family, sometimes his talk could even be taken as complaints and it was a disloyal thing to do. But he trusted Coleman. What Bud said to him would be understood. Nothing Bud said here at this cabin could ever hurt his family; nothing Coleman said could ever hurt Bud.

"You can't think of anything?"

"It makes me think of Dad in a different way, that's all. I never thought about what he'd get a good feeling from. He never told me . . ." Bud knew that was lame. He shouldn't have to be told, not about someone he'd lived in the same house with all his life. "Flying, I guess. I know he likes doing that."

"He gets up in the morning wanting to fly?"

"Sometimes, yeah, I imagine he does." Bud stopped working on his possum pelt, too absorbed in his thinking, in seeing his father. "He's really happy up there flying."

Now, alone in his bedroom, Bud began folding clothes and putting them in drawers, putting books onto shelves, scooping together loose papers. His father often said he was self-centered. Bud thought that meant selfish or egotistical; it made him feel bad about himself because he knew he did think about himself, about what he was, about what he liked to do or have or become. All his daydreaming seemed to start with "I," and his father clearly saw such a person as wrong. "I" — in school. Bud was not happy there. He couldn't talk to people, not easily. He felt awkward, funny-looking. He was afraid that boys in the class, in the halls, in the lavatory, laughed at him. He would have preferred to be invisible, to go to school and do the lessons, since that had to be got through, while being completely unseen. It had something to do with the feeling that no matter what was demanded of him, he would probably muff it. In early spring, lists were posted, the teams. Everyone had to try out, during gym classes. There were baseball teams, basketball teams, swimming teams; you had to try out for something and you could be put on a first or a second, even a third string. Bud walked into the gym office to check the lists of teams, posted on a door. He had to walk past the gym teacher and a knot of the athletic kids who hung out in the gym office. He read the lists, and the further he read, the surer he became that he shouldn't have bothered. His name wasn't anywhere, not even on a third string. He walked out and all of the people in the office were silent until he was out of the room, and then he heard them laughing.

Whenever Bud went down to the river to spend a whole Saturday in his boat or with Coleman, he knew there was a chance his father would call him selfish. Some chore left undone, or the failure ever to play with his little sister.

There are people who know how to work, to be practical, to accomplish things, Mac Taylor said. And Bud understood the rest of the equation: there are people who don't. He had begun to think of himself as well as of Coleman as one of the people who don't.

Bud stayed in his room. There he didn't have to see anyone's annoyance. Between the dog caught in the trap and the trouble over his trying to take the boat, Bud felt as though he had reached an especially low point. The only times Bud ever made his bed were times when he felt this way, felt the family didn't think much of him. Today the bed was made and the whole floor cleared. And all the time he was moving about the room, he was thinking about Coleman, seeing images of him, making up stories about Coleman leaving town to escape the flood or Coleman being rescued by Bud. When he thought of Coleman leaving, so that Bud would never see him again, he felt hollow and lonely. The picture of rescuing Coleman by boat was far happier. Bud spent all morning weaving and reweaving the images.

6

Bud heard the car leave while he was making his bed. When he heard it return, and the horn blow, he guessed that his mother had shopping bags. He ran out to the shed the Taylors used as a garage.

The back seat held a wall of paper grocery bags.

"I thought I ought to buy quite a lot? While we can still get to the stores?"

"Yeah. Oh, this is heavy!" Bud looked into a bag; cans.

"Beans, canned corn, chili; things we can eat if the electricity goes and we can't depend on the fridge," his mother said. "I am sorry it's so heavy."

Bud carried wet, loaded brown bags from car to kitchen.

At lunch, Mac Taylor said he had spent the morning in the city. Meetings, he said.

"Anything being done besides talk?" his wife asked.

Sara asked, "About what? The flood?"

"Pumps and sandbags distributed in threatened areas."

"Are we a threatened area?" Sara asked.

"Of course. Fire stations, radio stations, police, are all on alert. Trouble is, the mayors and chiefs of police are out of town in half the places, because it's Saturday. But the State Civil Defense set up an emergency center. They can bring in medical people. They'll distribute food. And there's a helicopter rescue service."

"Oh, Mac, you won't be flying?"

"No, Jean, I won't. No, my next job is to try to talk some sense into the people who live in areas where the flood is likely to go. I have to persuade them to get out."

"Where will they go, Daddy?" Sara seemed as pleased with the situation as her father.

"Shelters. The Emergency Center. The Red Cross will set up shelters. The church at the intersection out here may be used, though it seems like a dumb idea to me. You can see the stains on the church foundations from the big flood six years ago. Suppose this flood goes higher?"

"Higher than that one?" Bud's mother was picking her paper napkin to pieces. She seemed to do well when there were things to be done, but she became nervous when she listened to Mac talk about flood prospects.

"Higher," Mac said, comfortably. "There is a big high pressure area to the north, over the Gulf of St. Lawrence, and that is going to hold this storm right here."

"Oh, Mac." Bits of paper napkin dropped onto the table.

"Yup, everything points to the river beating past records. A lot of homes at the bend, the trailer park, maybe the old section up the river from here — they're all low and they're in for trouble."

"Daddy, will we be flooded?"

Bud thought Sara looked disappointed when her father replied, "No, baby, we're too high."

Jean Taylor said, "What about Rose and her mother? They thought their house would be above any floods."

Miss Rose Petersen and her aged mother had bought a new pink house, one in a tract with a fine view of the river, just as the newspaper advertisement had said. Miss Petersen taught history in the junior high. It had taken her years to earn a down payment on a house and this house had come high, considering its size and quality (Mac Taylor had said it wasn't built, it was thrown together) because of that view. It would be ironic if the river they paid so much to see became the destroyer of their house.

"Sure," Mac said. "I always told you a higher than normal flood could cut right under the fill that contractor put in there."

"But, Mac, that's just cruel."

Coleman's cabin, built on the rocks where normal spring waters rose, Coleman's crudely built home, had cost nothing, but its loss would surely be just as cruel,

Bud thought. He asked, "Isn't there some way to make dams, to deflect the water?"

His father laughed at him. "Bud wants to stop the flood again. Oh, sure, sandbags help, in some places. But we're not going to hold back much of this water, not even with sandbags."

Bud followed his father onto the porch to look at the river, misty and dark in the heavy rain.

There was snow high in the White Mountains, and the rain would be melting it. All the rivers that led into the Connecticut Valley carried extra loads of melted ice and snow by now. Water ran into the Ammonoosuc and into the Nash Stream, into the White River and into the Deerfield, and they all drained down into the Connecticut, swelling and swelling its volume. Mac Taylor talked about rivers and mountains and accumulating waters, as he stood on his porch. He reminded Bud of how the Farmington River had looked when they flew over it. "In town this morning, they said the Westfield River is already over its banks."

Bud pictured rain, like the rain that plowed the field in front of him, coming down all over Connecticut and all over Massachusetts and lower Vermont and New Hampshire, and he imagined rivers through all those states pushing, rising, steely and menacing like the water in their own river. He could not understand the undercurrent of jubilation he heard in his father's voice. He watched a tree branch ride past the river bank, and said, "There's a lot of power in the water, isn't there?"

"Yup. So be some use, Bud."

Mac dropped Bud off at the churchyard. A group of men and boys were milling about and Bud stood at the edges, waiting to be told what to do. A truck drove in and dumped a load of sand onto what was once green lawn lapped before the church doors. Men brought burlap bags out of the rectory. They picked up shovels and scooped sand into the bags. Shovels hit the cement walk, shrieking. Bud found a bag and shovel to work with; he took a place at the side of the sandpile. He held a bag open, shoveled, and tried to make the sand go into the bag. The bag would fall closed, the sand would flow outside the bag and back into the sandpile.

"Here, kid, you hold a bag and I'll shovel." The boy who spoke was huge, and he wore a motorcyclist's jacket. Bud disliked him immediately, but he held the bag open.

Another boy stood nearby, wiping rain from his glasses. He watched Bud and the boy in the motorcycle jacket for a moment. "We aren't going to stop any flood at this rate," he said.

Bud and the first boy together dragged an enormously heavy, filled bag and laid it against the foundation of the church. Bud seemed to end up doing the larger share of heavy work, while the boy, twice Bud's weight, told him what to do. "Put it farther over there"; "get the bag over that stone." After they had filled and dragged four more bags, Motorcycle Jacket said his arms ached and he wandered away, muttering about the stupidity of playing in sand. The boy in glasses offered to hold a bag for Bud to fill.

Rain flowed down over their heads and over the filled bags that looked small and useless leaning against the church basement.

"It's too slow," one of the men said. "It's too damn slow."

Bud remembered a toy he had had long ago, in a sandbox: a miniature conveyor. "There's a belt conveyor over in the quarry isn't there?" he said.

The man's head came up. "Right!" he said. "Jack!" he yelled to the man in the dump truck, who stayed dry and kept his cigar out of the rain in the truck cab. "That conveyor belt at the quarry, self-powered, isn't it? Go get it for us, Jack."

"What for?" came out of a puff of cigar smoke.

"Because a lot of people aren't working, Fat One. Haven't you seen? That river's up two more feet. We need these damn sandbags. Your house doesn't get any sandbagging until the church and Miller's store are secure."

The driver put his truck in gear and spun the tires in

mud. Someone chucked a shovelful of sand under the back wheels and the truck left. When it returned, a tractor followed with the conveyor. The conveyor had a hopper for loading crushed stone into trucks. The fat driver brought it down to a horizontal position. He started the engine. Then he got back into his truck which had been newly filled and sand poured from the dump truck to the hopper and off the end of the conveyor in a wide, fast stream. Men and boys yelled with pleasure. They lined up, holding bags. Now their problem was to move filled bags out of the way fast enough to keep up with the sand. Everyone was laughing and someone said to Bud, "That was an idea you had!" The boy with the glasses spoke. Bud laughed happily with them.

Gusts of wind blew from the northeast.

"Funny thing," Glasses said, "the wind comes out of the north and the radio said this storm was coming from the south. So maybe the storm is blowing away." He wore a wool cap and a wool plaid coat. Bud guessed both must be soaked through and heavy with the water they held.

"My dad says that even though the whole storm moves in from the south, you can be getting wind from the north. The center of this one must be near New York City, moving —" he pointed northeast — "that way." He wished his father were hearing this. He'd be pleased with Bud; that would make today just about perfect.

"Why doesn't this wind from the north blow the storm south?"

"A low goes across the country from southwest and west to northeast, Dad says. It has something to do with the rotation of the earth and the direction of jet streams. Those are stronger than the winds blowing within the storm."

They moved apart, dragging sacks of sand through the milling group of people. Back in line with empty bag in hand, the boy asked, "What's a low?"

Bud's arms and shoulders had begun to ache. He rubbed his back. "It's a storm area where the barometer reading is lowest at its center. Wind goes around counterclockwise in a low." Bud made a circular motion with his hand. "Like a Frisbee, it turns and moves along at the same time, I guess. As the storm approaches where you stand, the wind blows from the east and northeast, and after the storm center passes you, the wind is blowing from the west and northwest."

"So the center is still coming toward us?"

"Yup."

The boy nodded, as if glad to have the knowledge. He was tall, thin, with a wide, serious, flat face — at least two years older than Bud.

"I'm Michael," he said, and waited.

"Bud Taylor." Bud felt good. Not only Sara could find a friend; he had done it, too. The boy, Michael, wasn't loud, wasn't a show-off, wasn't teasing, wasn't any of the things Bud expected his classmates to be.

They dragged more bags of sand to the barricade that grew beside the old church. Bags were piled as high as the water stain from the flood of five years earlier. Sacks hid a long crack angling across the old stone foundations.

Rain had shortened the day. Already it was dusk. Bud walked back toward home. A sudden scream of wind, a hail of leaves and twigs stopped him. He watched, unbelieving, as a tree, the biggest of their oaks, something forever vertical, slowly moved its immense length to an angle, sinking until it rested against the side of the Freers' house. The telephone wire was down and snaked across the Taylors' yard.

Suddenly all noise ceased, as if his world were only connected with sound by a telephone wire. Bud stood still in the storm's caught breath. Like a gasp, an eerie moment, it was so silent it ought to have had some special meaning. Then the rains came again in a drumming curtain; wind shook leafless tree tops, and a truck in low gear ground its way up a hill.

Bud told himself he should go next door to call the phone company. The Taylors and Freers would be without a phone if he didn't. But he'd have to talk to Mrs. Hechler. She'd be arch and chummy.

Mac Taylor stopped Bud at the door. "Go phone Doctor Miller. Use the Hechlers' phone. Ours is dead and so is Freers'. I just hope Hechlers' works."

Bud felt wet and tired. His feet were cold. His arms ached.

"Go on! Mrs. Freer is having one of her spells."

Bud explained to Mrs. Hechler about the phone lines. She looked somehow smaller than usual, in spite of her tight pink slacks and stacked-up yellow hair. She forgot to ask him if he was "doing good in school"; she offered him no Pepsis this time. Instead, she held onto his arm and her voice went too high. "I'm so scared. I heard on the radio where it's going to be the worst flood in history. Did you hear that tree go down? I thought it was the atom bomb. And then everything just stopped. That was the worst thing I ever heard." Two small children clung to her pink pants, watching her face. One of them began to sob.

"Hey, it'll be okay, Mrs. Hechler," Bud heard himself say. "My dad and I are next door. We'll take care of you. Want to take the kids over to our house now?"

She clutched him again when she heard him tell Dr. Miller's receptionist that Mrs. Freer had chest pains. But he told Mrs. Hechler, when he hung up, "Mrs. Freer is just making herself sick being scared." He hoped she'd get the idea. "My dad and I are here. We'll look after you and the Freers. Thanks for letting me use the phone."

He left a pool of water on her floor. He had forgotten how wet he was. The Hechler child he carried through the rain to his home complained, "You're getting me all soaked." Mrs. Hechler ran behind him, carrying the other child. "Whew. It is wet, isn't it?" she said, when she reached the Taylors' kitchen.

His mother never blinked at the invasion. She seemed to have been waiting for it. She took their guests to sit by the open fire.

Bud dropped water-filled coat and pants and shoes on the bathroom floor. Even his underpants he could wring out. He took everything off and got between blankets in bed.

Late that night he woke, his stomach painfully empty. In the dark, he found his bathrobe on the floor and put it on. He stood in front of the open refrigerator, wondering what his family had eaten for dinner and if there was anything left for him, when his father came into the kitchen.

"Sara saved you her piece of steak. The Hechler kids ate yours. After a day like this one, you deserve a top-grade porterhouse steak."

Bud grinned at him. He found the cold meat. "Hechlers sleeping here?"

"Yeah, that woman is afraid to be alone."

"What's happening outside now, Dad?"

"Wind shifted to the north northeast." Mac carried a glass of milk into the living room where the barometer was. "Whew! This thing is low!"

Bud followed, and in the dim light from the kitchen, saw his father's face, gray under the eyes, strained, worried. Bud wondered if he would really be able to keep the storm from harming the elderly Freers and Mrs. Hechler or even themselves. For the first time in his life, he doubted his father's power. Not all the knowledge in the world about weather had been able to stop the flood.

7

The wind still blew on Sunday morning, a steadier wind, no violent gusts, and the rain, still heavy, had diminished. The air had a chill now, brought in by the west northwest wind.

A voice from a radio turned on loudly in the kitchen reported exceptional rainfalls had taken place on Saturday. Five inches had fallen in Connecticut and more in New Hampshire. The White River Junction–Lebanon section of the valley was already flooded and the river was over its banks in Massachusetts. Flood stage was expected to reach Hartford that day.

"It'll reach us tomorrow, then," Mac said, buttoning up a slicker.

The river was going to sprawl out and spread over farms and into basements. It couldn't be stopped. Bud put on his rain shirt.

He followed his father down to the river, a strange river, not his river anymore. Banks had been scooped away in places, as if sea monsters had taken bites out of the shore. Water had poured over low fields and was running among the trees and onto the road bordering the river.

"I thought you said tomorrow," Bud said.

"Wait till you see it tomorrow."

"Dad, couldn't I take the boat out for a little while?"

His father looked at him as if he had used an obscene word. "Do you know what your mother would say?"

"Yeah, but I can handle it, Dad."

"I doubt that. Besides, what's the point?"

There was no way now for Bud to tell his father about an old man living in a shack on a creek. "I just want to go," he said lamely.

"You're going to stay put," his father said.

They walked back toward the road and up along the place where the river made a snaking curve. Water ran over the foundations of three houses close to the banks. The houses looked like people standing up to their knees in a pond. That area was flooded every year. Owners and tenants hauled out their TV sets and bags of food, to move into the church every time. Bud saw two figures wading between the road above and an open front door. They were carrying bundles — maybe blankets.

In places, the shoulder of the road had turned into a deep gouge, full of running water. Bud and Mac walked a long way, looking at the effects of the storm.

"Hey, Able!" Mac called to a friend, a carpenter who lived in a small bungalow overlooking the river.

Mr. Able was lifting a rock. He got it off the ground and he moved, bent over his burden, to a ragged levee he'd been building. He dropped the rock among sandbags and dirt he'd heaped up to keep water out of his cellar. When he straightened, his face was dark red.

"Better take it easy," Mac said.

"Nope." The man began tugging at a fallen tree. "I didn't build this house by taking it easy. Besides, I've got my daughters and a wife in there to keep dry."

"Where do you want this thing?" Bud's father lifted the end of the tree trunk and motioned to Bud to help. Even with three pairs of arms raising it, the tree felt impossibly heavy to Bud.

"Up in my front yard," Mr. Able said. "We'll need it for heat if the electricity goes."

"Maybe you shouldn't stay here, Able," Mac said. He was looking down toward the river which already seemed closer than it had half an hour before. "You could bring your family along up to our house for the duration."

"And abandon my house? No sir, I built this house with these hands —" the hands almost too shaky to hold a handkerchief now — "and I'm not deserting it just for a storm."

"The river is going to keep rising."

"I know that. Just get me that tire iron I left down there, sir; used that to pry up a good-sized boulder for my dam here." His voice sounded weary.

Bud ran down the slope, sliding on slick grass, and retrieved the tire iron.

Then he and his father went on, but Mac Taylor said, as they walked away, "Bud, remind me to find out how they are tonight."

A pickup truck approached them on the road, sending up sheets of water from both sides. It slowed and stopped. Mac Taylor's flying friend, Joe Damico, stuck his head out. "I had to turn back. The bridge down there is out. How d'you like that?"

"No kidding! This is getting too big for fun."

Bud thought his father sounded delighted with the bigness.

"Yeah, I heard that the Farmington is really on the rampage; it's caused an unbelievable lot of damage. Half a town washed right down the main street. The Connecticut is over flood stage and it's still rising fast at Hartford."

"If the storm doesn't move out, and it keeps on dumping heavy rain all up the valley today and tonight, I'd say you could look for a crest to raise the present level another ten feet," Mac said.

Mr. Damico whistled.

"We are looking at a nightmare week ahead, until all that rain and melted snow gets past us and this river settles back."

Bud looked back toward Mr. Able's house. Four more feet and he would be awash. No homemade levee could hold back a ten-foot rise. He noticed the way the line of the porch on the side balanced the lines of the extra room built on the back of the house. He thought of Mr. Able hammering the nails into all those boards and then he thought about the river tearing them apart.

Beyond Mr. Able's small brown house, Bud saw — and heard — the river. A few days ago, it had moved placidly between well-defined banks. Before the storm, the river obeyed laws. Now it ran free. It did not have to follow plans; no order guided it. Like men who had gone mad and killed senselessly, slashing with knives, firing rifles into crowds, throwing bombs, lost to limits. The river was human, for Bud, benign, helpful, beautiful at times; now it seemed a different face of the human. Tree trunks swung and hurled along in the brown water, flashes of color on unidentifiable objects swirling in the foam, the mud caving in at the banks, these were the river's weapons of violence.

Bud shook himself and listened again to the two men.

". . . National Guardsmen and all the trucks they can round up will be evacuating those families. I've been driving truckloads of 'em all day. There's a levee upriver that threatens to collapse, too. Civil Defense is using boats and amphibian ducks and even helicopters, to get people out."

Maybe there was, after all, some way to find out how Coleman was doing; maybe the National Guard or Red Cross or somebody else doing rescue work would tell him. But Bud did not know whom to ask or how to reach people who knew. He just had to wait.

Waiting was especially hard on Sunday. All day, Bud's father kept him at his side. Obviously, Bud was not going to be trusted near the boat alone, not again. He looked back toward the river, now and then; wherever they went, he was within sight of the river. All day he heard its sound, which had become mighty and pervasive, a being he had to get used to having with him all the time. When he looked at the river, when he listened to the river, he thought of Coleman. He imagined himself — over and over the images rode with him — going down to the boat, untying the hawser, starting the motor, and getting out into the main sweep of the river, headed toward Coleman's creek.

He and his father walked down toward the washed-out bridge. Bud had expected to see the river flow over the center of the bridge, but what they found was that the bank on their side had been so undermined by the heavy pressure of water that the end of the bridge had collapsed. It was an old bridge, a narrow metal, one-lane bridge. Perhaps it had been rusty and weakened. Perhaps the water had been undermining that bank for years, with each spring's flood eating a little further under the bridge support. Now it had given way. People stood looking at it, as if they waited for something further to happen, or as if they wanted to remember this sight. It would be something to tell other people about someday. "Did you see the Old Mill Bridge? I did."

When his father suggested they help fill sandbags again, Bud's back ached in anticipation. Not again. Not more of that pulling heavy bags. But he found, once they began, that today he could do it more easily. He worked as part of a team with his father for a while. Then his father became impatient. Bud did not work fast enough, he said. So they separated. They filled bags and added them to other filled bags for three hours. Bud looked for Michael, the boy who had worked with him last time, but he did not find him.

The day became longer, harder to bear, during the afternoon, when Bud's father said they'd both have to take a break for a while, that it wasn't wise to exhaust themselves, and he disappeared behind the previous week's Sunday newspaper. Since no newspapers were delivered this Sunday, and since the Taylors kept weeks of old papers piled in the basement, Mac Taylor read a paper he must have read thoroughly seven days before. Bud watched his father reading and he thought it would be smart not to ever buy any more newspapers. The Taylors could just go on reading and rereading the cellar supply. What would it matter?

It occurred to him that people in other towns, in other states, were reading this Sunday's newspaper, and what they were reading about was what the Taylors were living through. Newspapers would print photographs of this river. Maybe a helicopter Bud had heard in the morning was up there to make films of the flood. How strange that people who lived far out of reach of the flood knew, already, more of the total picture of this flood than the people in the middle of it could possibly know.

Strange, too, to realize that those were not very exciting words — "flood," "homes damaged," perhaps "deaths." They were words that people would read while drinking their morning orange juice and coffee. Then they would fold up the paper, they would put it in the basement with other old papers, or use it to line a garbage can. As if the words did not have any connection with things that happened to living human beings.

Mac Taylor sat in the armchair that sagged in the seat so that it enclosed him in faded floral print. A standing lamp poured light down onto the paper. Mac wore his glasses down his nose when he read, pushed them back up whenever he looked up to speak to someone.

"Dad, I could go back to the bridge and take a picture of it. That would be some photograph to have."

Mac slid his glasses up and gave Bud a straight look. "You don't need to go out again," he said.

Bud knew what he was being told: he had tried to take the boat, against orders, and so today no move would be trusted.

He roamed the house restlessly. Books lay in small piles on tables; books leaned this way and that on shelves in his own room. Books meant a way to make whatever went on in the house unimportant. Bud could remove himself immediately into the worlds where other people lived other lives, just by picking up a book. But today that escape remained shut. The stories told between covers, in print on pages, had no power to answer the problem filling his head: what about Coleman? Bud lay on his bed. He turned on a reading light. He read a page. He wondered if he could slip down the backstairs and get out to the boat. He brought his mind back to the book, and read part of another page. How had he begun thinking of ways to do something behind the backs of his family? Well, hadn't everything about the friendship with Coleman been behind their backs? It had, but he'd never thought before that it was sneaking.

Bud sat up and stared out the window. He'd just walk downstairs and talk to his father about Coleman and his dad would understand and let him try to find the man. Oh, sure. Bud flopped back onto the pillows. Sure. Fat chance.

Maybe his mother? Bud went down to the kitchen and found her mopping the kitchen floor.

"Boy, Mom, you'd think there was enough water around without you putting some on our floor!"

His mother smiled at him, a tired smile. Bud realized that having had Mrs. Hechler and her children stay in the house the previous day had not made his mother's life easier. The Hechlers had gone back to their own house when the wind died down, but that did not remove the mess made by the children or the pots and pans in which their meals were cooked.

"Mom, did Mrs. Hechler help you in here at all?"

She shook her head and smiled again.

She looked startled when Bud took the mop handle out of her hands. "I can do this," he said.

He hated this kind of work, hated it even more than filling sandbags. But mopping, and later scrubbing a burned pan in which spaghetti had overcooked, and emptying garbage cans, and sweeping the back porch — these helped Bud work out that push that was in him to run down the back lawn and get into the boat. While he swept the porch, he watched the river. Under today's gray sky, the water ran, hard, slate-colored and slate-textured.

Bud never found a way to discuss Coleman with his mother.

8 "Shut up, can't you?" Mrs. Hechler slapped a child and he screamed and held his cheek.

The Hechlers had returned to stay — again — overnight. This time Mrs. Hechler was afraid of the river.

Mac Taylor looked at the woman and at the crying child over his glasses, and went back to the newspaper. Today he was reading the previous Monday's paper.

Bud's mother brought a platter from the kitchen and the sound of the radio followed her through the open door. All the faces at the breakfast table turned toward that sound.

". . . and during the past twenty-four hours, the river has risen eight feet at Hartford, the highest rise on record here for one day."

Mac pushed his glasses back and stood up. "Crest will hit late tomorrow. I've got to get people out of their houses before it's too late." Now Bud heard in his father's voice the same tension he had felt inside himself for days. "You check the boat and tie it higher, Bud." He was to be trusted today?

A fine rain fell, and the clouds were lighter and higher and showing signs of breaking. The radio had reported a forecast for clearing later that day. Bud pictured the storm as having got loose from that blocking high, to whirl off over Nova Scotia and on northeastward, taking its rains out of New England, now that it had left behind a trail of disaster. The river was closer to their house than before. The top of their dock was a dozen feet underwater. Water spread across low-lying land on the other side of the river. Two houses over there were up to their windows in water. That would put it well over the chimney of Coleman's shanty, Bud guessed.

Out of the main channel and over this flooded area, the water ran more slowly than it did in the center; it was not the swirling torrent that was the main body of the river. Bud believed he could manage the boat if he could stay in this overflow. Somehow today he was going to get to Coleman's stream. Today he would make sure Coleman was safe. That the old man might have been unable to get away from the river, that he could be hurt, stranded — these fears flowed through Bud like the sweeping dark water.

Thanks to the long hawser, the boat was still within reach. She rode low, heavy with rainwater. Bud spent fifteen minutes bailing. Then he had trouble starting the motor. Finally, it sputtered and came to life. Just don't let the sound bring anyone to a window up in the house, he thought. If they saw him and tried to stop him, there would be no getting to Coleman. This had to be done. Tight with hurry — don't let them hear, don't let them stop me — he headed the boat downstream, crabbing close in and away from the main body of the river.

Along one stretch, new houses had been built just above past flood levels. Now they were in water. Somewhere in the neighborhood would be the Shrivers' house. Bud had seen Mr. Shriver last Saturday morning for a short time, among the men working on sandbags. Then he'd gone. The Shrivers must have left their riverside house and moved in with relatives or friends somewhere else. They had four small children and a grandmother who lived with them. Their house, weathered wood above a stone foundation, must have seen many floods, Bud thought, but none this high.

He put the engine in reverse to control the boat around some floating junk. Once she caught on something down in the darkness of the water and, slewing around abruptly in the current, tipped until water began to come in over one side. Again Bud reversed and got loose. He had not wanted anyone to look out the window at home when he was leaving, but now he rather wished his father could see the way he was handling the boat. He had relaxed; he felt very much in control. He was managing just the way he was sure Mac Taylor would manage.

Bud saw what he thought was the Shrivers' house. But it couldn't be; it was too small. How could he get his bearings in this strange landscape of trees and buildings that stood in a fast flow of river? Then he recognized the roof, its shingles loose and in need of repair, the way they always seemed to be. He steered carefully to the downstream side and up under a second-floor window.

A face came into view and then moved back and then came forward, smiling and smiling.

Bud was used to the river without people, his river. Now the floods had created a strange world that seemed to have nothing at all to do with the lives of towns and streets, schools and families. The river was, now, even more remote than usual from ordinary life. The sound of the river was so tremendous that it blanketed all the normal sounds, the trucks, the church bells, the barking and shouting and car gears shifting. This face in a window shocked him.

Old Grandmother Shriver was rocking in her rocking chair and waving to him.

Bud caught hold of a shutter and pulled the boat in close. He knocked on the window and then the woman stopped her chair and opened the glass.

"My, how nice of you to drop by, Buddy Taylor. I was wondering if someone might stop by, but I really didn't think many folks would be getting about today."

"Mrs. Shriver, where's your family?"

"Won't you come in?" She would not be serious. "The folks went off Saturday, Saturday morning it was, and they haven't got back yet. I expect they think I've stayed at my sister Milly's. You come right on in. It's a little wet over the floor, but I've kept my feet dry by sitting in my rocker."

Bud tied the boat to a shutter hook and hung on to the windowsill.

"Isn't the river a sight?" she was saying, and Bud saw that her floor was damp and in places puddled. "I watched the most remarkable sight a little while ago. One of those new houses they put up across the way there, I saw it slide, just like a ship being launched, right off into the river, and it floated a bit as if it thought it could be a ship, and then it began to come all apart and there have been pieces of house going past my window ever since. That contractor who put those little houses up, he could be collecting the pieces downstream somewhere to put up another lot of the things. I don't imagine they'd be any worse than what he built here."

Bud said, "I'll take you over to dry land, Mrs. Shriver." He hated saying those words. Now he could not go on to look for Coleman. Once he got home, his father would never let him out of sight again. "We'll get you to your family," he said. "You can't stay here."

"Well! This is exciting, being rescued from a second-story window!"

Bud said, "Come on, please, Mrs. Shriver." She would take all day, he thought.

"Can you hold that boat of yours in tight? I don't believe I want a swim in such cold water."

"I'll hold her steady. Can you climb out the window?"

"Just as soon as I get my jacket on." She was rummaging about in a closet and then came back with a coat over her arm. "Now you look the other way while I put my legs over the windowsill."

"Take my hand, Mrs. Shriver." To Bud, she seemed so small, her hands tiny birdclaws in his hands. "Put your feet on the seat, as near the middle of the seat as you can."

Her short legs just barely reached the seat. He braced her arms, taking her weight — of which there was very little. Then she was there, sitting in the boat with him, smiling cheerfully.

Bud let the boat drift a little away from the house. Then he turned it against the current with the motor full ahead. Even far from the main body of the river, the flow of the water was powerful and the boat seemed to make poor headway. Slowly, they progressed. They passed a floating outhouse. Then they went by the roof of a long shed projecting above the water. A wet, shivering dog sat on the roof and whined.

"We'll have to rescue that dog, won't we, Buddy?"

All Bud wanted was to get Mrs. Shriver out of the flood, back to land quickly. He wanted to leave her somewhere warm and safe, and then to look for Coleman. But she insisted on getting the dog. Bud was annoyed. She treated the flood like a tea party. One more guest, that was all. Bud gritted his teeth. It took time to bring the boat to the shed; it meant losing some of the headway they had made. Bud slid the boat close to the roof. The dog saw its chance and jumped.

"He's so glad to be with us." Mrs. Shriver petted him and murmured to him, and the dog lay down at her feet.

Bud took them to the place where the Taylors' dock had been. He had the strange experience of running his boat directly above the dock. He could look down through murky water and see its boards below. He helped the woman and the dog ashore, easing the woman gently, while holding the dog back, and then giving the dog a boost that sent him where he obviously wanted to be — at Mrs. Shriver's side.

He'd wait, he thought, until she reached the house. Then he could cut out and get down to the stream and see where the cabin had gone. But the tiny woman climbing the hill stumbled. Bud tied the boat as quickly as his hands could work the rope around a tree trunk, and ran after her. He put a hand under her elbow, the way he'd seen his father support his grandmother, and he felt her trembling. She took the steep backstairs to the kitchen door one by one, her fingers a fierce grip on Bud's arm.

For a while she sat on a straight chair not moving or speaking, her face masklike. Bud's mother put a sweater around her shoulders. Bud's father handed her a shot glass of brandy.

"How long were you up there alone, Mrs. Shriver?" Jean Taylor asked. She stood at the stove, stirring soup.

"This morning," Mrs. Shriver said. She sipped brandy and roused herself, as if from a sleep. "When I looked down the stairway, I saw water part way up. That hallway was such a grand swimming pool. I wasn't quite ready for a swim just then, so I went back to my room and settled down to wait. I watched all that water go by on all sides. It was a show! Yesterday, there was a lot of water then, too. And rain, was that the day before? I never did see it rain so hard, did you?"

"You had nothing to eat all that time?"

"I did nicely. A bag of temple oranges was tucked away in my room. They are so good! I must say I am grateful for this." With the brandy, color returned to her cheekbones and her determined alertness came back with it.

Bud's mother took away the glass. She drank a glass of sherry, once in a long while, with Mac, but when she did, she talked a lot about how dangerous alcohol was. Bud guessed that her talk was always for his benefit, as if she were afraid he would begin drinking and hanging around taverns if she didn't say those things.

"Get yourself something hot to drink, Bud," his father said. "You did a real job out there on the river." And, quickly, before Bud had time to enjoy the praise in his father's voice, "Better feed that dog, too."

Bud gave the dog a lamb bone he found in the refrigerator. That was when he noticed that the electricity was out. No light came on inside the refrigerator. No wonder the kitchen had seemed gloomy.

He wondered when his mother was going to mention his having taken the boat. But she had a full kitchen and a real emergency and real worries. She could make soup on a gas stove, but only so long as the supply of food held out, and without refrigeration what they had was not going to keep for long.

Bud started for the kitchen door. There would still be time to get out on the river. But Mac Taylor came back into the kitchen. "Empty the buckets we've put in the bedrooms, will you, Bud."

"Buckets?"

"Sure. Roof's leaking all over the place."

Bud despaired of getting out again in the boat.

The Taylors ate dinner by candlelight. Outside, broken clouds allowed glimpses of a moon. The house, with its electricity out, seemed special, warmer and closer than usual, to Bud. The Hechler children had been fed early and put to bed. Mrs. Hechler was subdued, perhaps tired out from her fears. Mrs. Shriver nodded and smiled and said very little, as if she too were worn out. Bud's mother had brought out a collection of candle stubs. They dripped into jar lids on the table and the sideboard, and the light softened all the faces.

After dinner, Mac took Mrs. Shriver to the church to look for her family. Jean Taylor sent Bud with an orange crate full of kindling and Sara with a box of new candles to the Freers' house. The elderly couple had no light at all. Bud built a fire for them, and when it caught, the little parlor seemed less chilly. Mr. and Mrs. Freer sat desolately, side by side, on the couch in front of the hearth and asked Bud to take them away. They had no idea where, just away from the storm. Bud told them the worst was over and that his father would make sure they were safe. They looked frightened when he and Sara left.

The family sat in candlelight, no television and only a small portable radio bringing the outside world to them. Mac said he'd heard the Connecticut Air National Guard had dropped food from a C-47 to a town in the western part of the state.

"Why did they do that?" Sara asked. She had made herself a nest of blankets and dolls on the floor under the big round table.

"Roads cut off. Bridges all down. No other way to get help to them," Mac said.

"Since the electricity's gone out, people are down at Miller's dairy farm milking the cows by hand," Jean Taylor said. "Seems kind of nice."

"They're the lucky ones." Mac shielded a candle as a sudden spurt of wind blew the flame over. Windows rattled. "Miller is on high ground. Some farms lost all their livestock."

"Drowned?" Bud heard the sharpness in his mother's voice. "Why didn't they get those animals to safe places?"

Mac said, "Take it easy, Jean. That's a huge job, moving a lot of livestock."

"Yes, but you told me the entire contents of some factories — machinery, goods, everything — were taken out and stored in dry places."

"Sure. Millions of dollars' worth."

"Dollars, not lives! How much do they value people?"

"They're trying, Jean. The National Guard has been flying in doctors and nurses to hospitals along the flood area. Civil Defense and Red Cross are sheltering people, doling out food, taking care of the injured."

Mac groped his way through the dark living room carrying the radio wherever he went. Music came in, thinly, taking them to some place distant from the flood. But the concerto ended and an announcer began to talk about water. Civil Defense shelters . . . a central disaster headquarters . . . Bud's mother look startled. It was as if Mac had used the radio to reinforce his argument.

The announcer said troops were out on some city streets and that one man had been shot attempting to loot a store. In Winsted, northwest of Hartford, the Mad River had gouged a six-foot canyon down the town's main street. Cars had been tossed about like toys, and the business section was ruined. One four-story building was turned askew on its base.

He described people waiting for rescue on rooftops, shouting to helicopters, "Give us milk," "Get us off," "We need food."

Fire had broken out in a mill, he said, and since there was no way for fire-fighting equipment to reach it, the historic old mill burned to the ground. A wrecked bridge had dammed water, so highway department officials brought in the National Guard to blow up the bridge.

"Turn it off," Bud's mother said, "turn it off. I don't want to know any more. What can we do? If they'd tell us how to be useful, how to protect people . . ."

How to protect Coleman, Bud thought.

"Let's wash up the dishes," Mac said, snapping off the radio. They boiled water in four pots on the stove and used that water for soaping and rinsing the dinner dishes. While Bud moved back and forth between the stove and the sink, working silently with his parents, he thought about Coleman. Maybe the old man had gone to one of the churches where beds were being set up. Maybe he was showing kids there how to draw a river rat.

9

What a way to spend a spring vacation. If only the flood had come a week earlier or a week later, these days would be missed from school. Bud resented the lost time on the river; he'd done a lot of planning that winter for the time he'd have in spring vacation. Now water was pouring over his plans. Tuesday was clear and colder, but above freezing. Bud's father went out to deliver water, clean drinking water, brought as far as roads were open in tank trucks, and carried, in plastic bottles, to homes out here in the flood area. Jean Taylor's fears had not been without reason, for by now cesspools had backed up and the water that ran from taps was contaminated. People were being told to boil their water. The trouble was, Mac said, some people had no gas or electricity for boiling anything.

Mac drove Bud to the main road to the city, and left him with a group of men trying to clear a tree and a mass of mud and rocks off the highway. With them was the boy with glasses who had filled sandbags on Saturday.

"Hey, Bud!" he called, as if he were glad to see him again.

"Hi, Michael."

The two shoveled side by side, feet slipping in wet clay soil that was smeared across the concrete pavement.

"Must have been something to see, that entire bank, mud, rocks, tree and all, come sliding down onto the road," Michael said.

"Scary."

There were acres of mud to be cleaned away. Eventually Bud's hands burned from his grip on the shovel's handle. His back began to ache.

"Tobacco fields upriver got four feet of water on 'em," a man said, and shovels squealed metal on cement.

"Yep. Farms being ruined this time. Much worse than any flood I can remember."

"That old barn down to Merry's Landing, that just floated away. I seen it go. And between here and two days ago, I hear five people been drowned, just in these parts."

"Five people!"

The men talked among themselves as they shoveled. Bud wondered if their news were true. He did not want to know that five people died in this flood. If only he could have taken the boat and looked for Coleman. But his father had said the road must be cleared, and he'd given Bud no chance to slip out to the boat. Strange, Bud thought, how no one in the family mentioned the way the boat was taken and Mrs. Shriver rescued. No one praised him for that, either. It simply disappeared, as if the good and evil he had done canceled out each other. Now he was forced to work here because his father asked: how would ambulances and fire equipment get through with the main road blocked? "Your own home could burn to the ground," Mac had said. So Bud was shoveling mud.

"That river's still rising," a man said. "Like there is no end to it coming up."

"Another man died, not by drowning," someone said. "It was heart attack."

"We guys better watch it!" A ripple of laughter followed.

Late in the morning, Bud rested on his shovel. His stomach growled. "Michael," he said, "want to come back to my house and eat?"

This was new for Bud Taylor. He had lived all his life assuming that he and his house would be of no interest to other people. He had gone to school and spoken, diffidently, to other people, and made a few friends without ever being sure they were really friends, and he had not asked anyone to his house. This time, Bud was so hungry he had stopped thinking about the flood because he couldn't think about anything except his stomach. Michael would be just as hungry. So it came out naturally: "Want to come back to my house and eat?"

"Sure; it's got to be closer than where I live."

Bud and Michael put their shovels into the road crew's truck, grinned at the friendly shouts and jokes of the men, and started toward the river. Traffic could get through the highway now, if the bridge at this end didn't get washed out.

"My dad says the storm center is headed off toward Nova Scotia by now." Bud had come to think of that low as a personality. It had threatened; it had issued warnings. It had rushed in and angrily hurled things, kicked and screamed, and then it had grown serious. There had been executions while the terrible rage of the storm was in full power. Now it had moved off, coldly indifferent, and left a people shuddering.

"If the storm is that far away," Michael said, "the flood must be over."

"No way. Rain was still coming down, hard, in New Hampshire all day yesterday. The river is flooded all the way up to Canada. It's going to be days before all that water moves through here. I guess hundreds of families will be taken out of their homes to get away from the river."

"Hundreds? I keep forgetting it isn't just here. Think of floods for miles and miles around us!"

They walked along the empty road in the sunshine, its warmth on their backs.

Michael pointed down the hill. "Look at that!"

Miss Petersen's house was only feet above the river

now. The real estate agent could say she had her view of the river today. The rushing current had risen and gouged away dirt and rock that was the fill under the little split-level. The house had slipped sideways; it tilted toward the water, poised to slide in.

Bud and Michael ran the rest of the way down the road and banged on the door. No one answered. They tried the knob and found it unlocked. Bud called into a damp hallway. No one replied.

"They've left. It's a good thing." He set the latch so the door would lock, and pulled it shut. The gesture seemed strange; he had locked the door so that the house could fall to pieces in the river, undisturbed by burglars. Bud had been taught that when you leave a house empty, you lock the doors. It seemed pointless now.

"I wonder if the trailers are in trouble," Michael said.

"What trailers? Park's Trailer Park?"

"Yes. I live there."

The place by the river where the children slid down the muddy banks to the river's edge. "You must be in my school district," Bud said. "But I don't remember seeing you."

"I quit school," Michael said.

Bud's father passed them in his car, stopped, backed up.

"Have you heard anything about Park's Trailer Park?" Bud asked, as he held the seat for Michael to get in back. "This is Michael. He lives there."

"Hi, Michael. We'll see if we can find out about Park's. Maybe you better spend tonight at the church, Michael."

"Nobody could stay sane there, if they've put all those little kids, fighting and running around, and all those mothers to bawl at them and scream at each other, together in one place," Michael said.

Bud and his father both laughed. "Spend the night with us," Mac said.

"I already asked him to eat with us," Bud said.

His father looked over at him, surprised.

All afternoon, Michael and Bud helped Mac Taylor deliver bottles of water, collect more bottles, and deliver those. All over the county, frightened people were grateful for the water; others did not believe in the danger. "Ah, what's to worry? I been drinking it all day, hasn't bothered me a bit." Mac would try to explain, and they'd wave the water away, or accept the bottles with a sneer and a shrug.

Food was spoiling in the Taylors' refrigerator. Bud's mother made a soup that was mostly vegetables she had stored in the basement: carrots, onions, turnips, potatoes. There was nothing to drink but boiled water, which tasted dull to Bud. Dinner dishes were washed in boiled water. All tasks were more difficult than usual, as the family worked by candlelight. For Bud it was a burden just to stand up, putting dishes into soapy water, taking them out. Suddenly he was more tired than he could remember ever being before. He found it intolerable to have to move across the kitchen floor, to have to answer when people spoke. His legs were so weary that his shoes felt extraordinarily heavy; his tongue felt thickened. He dropped a planter and it broke. "Sorry," he said, "I guess I am tired."

Sara said to Michael, "He breaks things a lot."

"No, he doesn't," Mac said.

Bud looked at him quickly, grateful for this.

Mike helped Bud set up a cot in Bud's room, shrinking the small space. They both threw books and clothes and whatever else littered the floor into the closet and shut the door, laughing because at first the door wouldn't shut and then, when it did, they could hear the piles of jumbled things falling against the door inside the closet.

"All those books," Michael said. "You like that stuff?"

"Some of it," Bud said. He resisted the temptation to say what many kids at school said, that they hated all reading, all schoolwork. With someone else he would have said that; but he liked Michael. "How could you quit school so early? You're not sixteen, are you?"

"Fourteen. And it isn't because I was flunking or anything like that. But nobody noticed; I guess they thought I'd moved."

They made up a cot. Bud tossed the pillow at Mike. "You had some reason for quitting?"

"Sure. I couldn't earn enough just working the kinds

of jobs kids can get after school. I bused dishes in the Circle Restaurant." Bud knew the place. It looked run-down, the lights always half out on the neon sign. "And some days they'd tell me they didn't need me. I'd walk all the way there after school and they'd say they didn't need me. So that day I wouldn't earn anything. Then I pumped gas at a gas station. But it closed. I've tried some other after-school and Saturday jobs; they just never earn enough real money. So I quit school."

Michael put his glasses on Bud's bureau and stretched out with his hands behind his head while Bud got into pajamas.

"You want to borrow a pair?" Bud asked him.

Mike laughed. He was six inches taller than Bud.

"How does your family take it, your leaving school?"

"I didn't discuss it with them."

"Didn't they bring it up? I mean, do they know you're not in school?"

Mike shrugged. "You talk about everything you do with your parents?" He had a squint when he didn't wear his glasses.

Bud lay in bed, but he didn't turn out the light for another two hours. He began to talk to Michael about Coleman. "I don't talk about quite everything with my family," he said. Bud had thought he would keep Coleman entirely a secret. But he liked telling Michael, he liked the way Michael listened, as if he understood how important the old man and the river and the trapping were. Finally, with his eyelids trying to close, and his words slowed by sleepiness, Bud was saying, "I tried to take the boat to go look for him, to see if he'd gotten away from the flood, but Dad stopped me, and I tried again and that time I had to fetch an old lady instead. He just can't still be down there. The cabin is bound to be washed away. Only I just have to go see. Maybe he moved the shack up to higher ground. Maybe he needs help. He could be hurt. He'd sure have trouble getting food, wouldn't he? Probably he left and went to stay somewhere else. I might be able to find some of his things floating around. I'd keep them for him until he gets back."

Michael never interrupted; he just listened. But he was awake, he was hearing. He even got up and put on his glasses, as if being able to see made his hearing better.

"It's driving me crazy. I've got to find out. Dumb, isn't it?"

"No," Michael said. "What's dumb about it?"

10

Wednesday morning was bright, cool, and sunny. Wind, what there was of it, was out of the west and the barometer was rising.

Michael stood by Bud's bedroom window, staring out at the boiling, furious river. "Couldn't we get there by land, hike or something?"

"Get there?"

"To the place where your friend lives. We ought to try."

Bud heard that "we." "There's no going by land that I know of, especially not now. Where he is will have water all around it. We'll have to take the boat."

"Look at that river!"

Bud came to the window. "Look at our land!"

Water covered the lower quarter of the property. The river seemed to have leaped toward the house during the night. Surely it would reach its crest today.

"We can't go anywhere in that," Michael said.

"I have to. I'm going to find out about Coleman and I'm going to do it today."

"Okay," Michael said. "Let's go."

Michael and Bud could hear the family and their other guests in the kitchen. They could smell the coffee brewing. But they did not stop. They went down the hill to the boat, which was riding halfway up the trunks of the trees that stood in the middle of the Taylors' weedy slope.

Bud untied the hawser. Then he heard his mother's shout. She ran toward them. Mrs. Hechler was stumbling down the hill after her, which struck Bud as odd.

"Stop!" His mother was breathless and Bud waited to be told he was a fool. "Bud, Mrs. Hechler just had a call from the Ables. Go up and get him. In the boat. His road is out. Can you two manage the boat in this? I'll call an ambulance and it'll be waiting here when you get back. Your father's already left to help down at the church."

Bud thrust his weight against the ground and pushed the boat away. As the engine caught, he shouted, "What's wrong with Mr. Able?"

Mrs. Hechler spoke in little gasps, an incoherent stream of words Bud couldn't make out over the motor.

"What did she say?" he shouted to Michael.

Michael shrugged and began bailing out rainwater.

Bud held the boat in over the flooded area, wary of floating trees and debris coming down the river. A doll carriage floated past. Michael pointed and Bud shivered. The carriage had not carried a real child, but the sight chilled them. Then they saw the body of a dead cat in the water. A muskrat, flooded out of his home, was being swept along close to the edges, scrabbling at roots and bushes as he passed them, and then he was yanked away out of sight by the strength of the river.

Bud kept on, headed upriver toward Ables', but his thoughts turned the other way, downstream to Cherry Creek where a small shack had stood just above a pebbly bit of beach. Where would the man be?

The motor spluttered. "Don't die. Don't die, you motor." Bud fought to keep the nose headed in the right direction.

Then they were in a section where the water moved more slowly. A bend in the river threw the faster water toward the opposite side. Bud maneuvered around a shed half under water. They crossed what he knew was a road that ran from the main highway to a dock. How strange to cross a road in a boat!

From there, it was slow going. At times Bud felt as if the efforts of the motor made no difference at all; surely they were not moving. But inch by inch the trees that stood in the water were passed. Bud thought of Mr. Able lifting huge rocks to protect his home, and he wondered what had happened. An ambulance — for Mr. Able? He also wondered how long it was going to take to get him back to the house. His mother's tone had been panic. An ambulance, image of speed, would have to wait absurdly while this boat poked its slow way in the river.

Able's house came in sight. Water had risen to the first floor level. All that labor to build a levee had been for nothing.

A woman Bud did not at first recognize came out and stood at the back door in boots, wearing a man's coat and a scarf.

"What's wrong?" Bud asked, as soon as he'd brought the boat in close and cut the motor.

"Talk later," the woman said. It was Mrs. Able. "Help me get him."

Michael stayed with the boat. Bud followed Mrs. Able into the house. They waded through three inches of water across the floor of the kitchen. Mr. Able lay on a bed and blood stained large areas of the daybed cover. A bloody dishtowel encircled his wrist. Three little girls around Sara's age and younger stood beside the bed, looking white and pinched with fright.

Bud and Mrs. Able helped Mr. Able out of the house. He said nothing. The man and woman got into the boat.

"How about the kids?" Bud asked.

"They'll have to stay and look after the house," Mrs. Able said.

Not until the motor was running again did she explain further, shouting over the noise. "I was helping Able to split a stump. We were up above the house. He wanted to cut it up for our stove because the furnace is flooded. So we were using the chain saw because you'd never split that huge old stump with an ax. That blade hit the bottom and leaped back and it got him in the wrist." She had made a tourniquet on Mr. Able's arm. Bud glanced at the man. How long can an artery flow? Would Mr. Able bleed to death? Was he going to die right here in this boat? Bud clenched his teeth, making his jaws ache, as he realized it was all up to him. Just Bud.

The wind and the power of the water suddenly clutched at the boat. Bud steered, intent on avoiding debris in the water. A heavy wooden crate tumbled ahead of them; if it hit the boat, they could all be thrown into the water. It's my job, Bud thought, mine. I have to do it. The boat must be held near shore. If it were swept out into the middle of the river, Bud would completely lose control of steering, he was sure. He tried heading with the current and putting the engine in reverse. It worked, but maneuvering wasn't easy. He could cut across the flooded fields, but the tops of submerged fences showed just at the surface of the water, and those could overturn the boat. That way seemed even more dangerous than the edges of the river, where boxes, branches of trees, even furniture, rushed and fell and disappeared and reappeared in the violent water. So he headed back with the current, at a furious speed, and at times he was sure it was the water, not he, that was in control.

Mr. and Mrs. Able huddled together. Bud could see the side of the woman's face. Her mouth was twisted to one side in fear. Michael's whole way of sitting, hunched forward with his hands on the gunwales, expressed tension. Bud tightened his hand on the tiller, feeling the boat's shudder in his palm. He had to keep his mind on exactly what he was doing; if he let his own fear come up to the surface, they would all drown.

In only five minutes he recognized the road to the shore. Their rush downstream had been so swift — and they had not yet left the shelter of the curve in the river — that Bud was afraid to keep on. Not with the responsibility of an injured man who could not swim if the boat went over. He swung around, heading against the current, with the motor in forward speed, and went at a crab angle away from the river. If he could just keep it over that road while he slowly headed for higher ground, he could get Mr. Able to someone who would send for the ambulance.

The small boat came in to the lee side of a building where boats were stored in winter. The water was quiet here, and Bud sagged with relief.

"Pretty shallow, isn't it?" Michael said.

"Would you check with the oar?"

The oar didn't go far down, so Bud cut the engine. Michael pushed the boat on up another twenty feet, to steps leading up to a house. He took the line ashore and pulled in, and together he and Bud half-lifted Mr. Able out and helped him up the steps.

The house belonged to a Swiss carpenter. Even though everything along the river had a disconcerting strangeness since the high water had erased landmarks or shifted them, Bud knew this house because there was always, even today, a flagpole with two flags, one Swiss and one American. The carpenter, a man with a small mustache, opened his door. His eyes went round when he saw Mr. Able being helped up his steps.

"I'll phone Mrs. Hechler to send that ambulance down the river road," the carpenter said.

Mr. Able put a hand on Bud's arm. His face was ashy gray. "Thank you," he said. "You did it."

11

Bud and Michael went back to the boat.

"Shall we try to get back? I didn't dare with Mr. Able so badly hurt. We could get thrown upside down so easily with all that junk tearing along in the water, and he couldn't possibly swim."

"Could we?" Michael asked.

"Oh, I guess. I still want to try to get down to Coleman."

"So stop delaying."

The current close to shore carried the boat around the bend, and then the river took over. At this rate, Bud thought, they'd be passing his own house in five minutes. A violent current poured south and the small motorboat was a mere twig to it. Bud remembered a time when he was four or five years old and he stood on a small bridge and dropped little sticks into the water. Then he'd run to the other side of the bridge to see them rush past.

The boat no longer responded to his direction at all; it

swung and careened faster than Bud had ever driven it. They came to the Taylor property. They passed it. Then, for a moment, Bud was so afraid that he was shivering uncontrollably. As long as he had had to use his whole mind and his whole body, pouring everything into getting the boat safely through, he had had no time for fear. Now that there was no longer anything he could do, he began to tremble.

Strange objects fell through the water with them. Bud saw a woman's shoe go by. An umbrella, most of the fabric torn from the frame, tossed up into sight and then disappeared. And, always threatening the boat, tree stumps, logs, remains of small docks tumbled in the current. Then the body of a drowned dog surfaced and slowly rotated as it moved past.

Bud and Michael looked at each other. Bud saw the sickness and also fear in Michael's face. He shook himself; he couldn't just let go. He would let the river take the boat down to Cherry Creek and then, somehow, get it out of the current. At least he was thinking again.

Beyond the water that boiled brown and ugly over the land, there was a house with water up to a dormer window in its roof. Another house close to the first was better off, though the floor of the first story was underwater. Above that house, a pickup truck lay on its side and an old garage was half caved in.

The flood was a monstrous fist that had smashed into the countryside, blind and brutal. What had it done to the fragile little cabin of Coleman, or to the man himself?

He recognized the entrance to the creek ahead. Now he must act. Now, or the chance would be gone. He tried to cut the boat across the current, but the slightest turn of the bow at any angle across the direction of the water heaved the boat and threatened to overturn it.

"That thing is headed straight at us!" Michael's shout rode over the roar of the river. A heavy eight-by-eight beam charged down the river toward the boat.

Bud could not worry now about getting into Cherry Creek. He had to do something to get them out of the way of that hunk of lumber. He swung the tiller and the boat whirled so fast that he could not keep his hands on the stick. Then the beam hit, smashing into the side of the motorboat.

Michael and Bud were thrown into the air and completely out of the boat. Something in the water hit Bud's arm and he felt it crack, a sickening feeling and very definite; he knew his arm was broken.

He swam with the one good arm, watching the junk that tossed and churned and rushed past him in the water. He found his own boat close to him and paddled toward it, but the boat was moving fast. Then some current caught both him and the boat, bringing him close enough to grab the side, jerking his hurt arm as he did so, sending sharp pain crashing up the arm. The odd current swept Bud and the boat straight at the bank.

"Michael!" he yelled. But the noise of the river mocked his puny shout.

People were suddenly there, men in boats, men standing on ground above water, men wading out across the flooded fields. Bud wondered why, and shouted for Michael again. Hands lifted him out of the water and he yelped when his broken arm was touched. Someone said, "You're hurt," and then he was passed into the arms of another person. "Watch how you carry him; something's broken." A blanket was wrapped around him very gently. Only then did he realize how cold he was. His teeth began chattering.

"Michael," he said. "Michael's out there in the water."

"The other kid? No, he's okay. We got him in already."

They set him on the ground and made him run, fast, to a jeep, and then he was driven away, with the blanket still around him and his jaw tense from so much shivering. The jeep bounced across the field, climbed a slope, reached a road. The driver had red hair and a reddish beard, and he kept looking over at Bud to make sure the bouncing of the jeep wasn't hurting him.

When they came to a stop, the driver of the jeep put an arm around Bud to keep the blanket from falling off, and led him into a firehouse. The place was full of people. Some lay on cots; some sat wrapped in army blankets like the one around Bud. Bud found a folding chair next to a man who sat hunched under a blanket, his nose running, and his cheek scratched.

"What is this place?" Bud asked him through chattering teeth.

"First aid station."

"Get those wet clothes off him," a woman ordered, and the jeep driver helped Bud ease his coat off the broken arm. Together they worked the shirt over it, too. Then Bud got out of the rest of his clothes and dropped them, sodden with water, onto the floor. A dry blanket wrapped around him felt warm and reassuring.

A different woman came with a cup of broth. "You must be the other boy from that motorboat."

"Where's Michael?" Bud asked her, trying not to shiver.

"In the kitchen, getting some soup."

Michael came, holding a steaming cup, through the crowded room, with someone else's jacket and overalls too loose on his thin frame. Bud laughed, shakily, and Michael said, "They're a better fit than your pajamas would have been. This is a mess."

"What's a mess?"

"These are all people from the trailer park." Michael stood awkwardly in the loose overalls, holding the warm cup with both hands and staring down into it. He met Bud's look, finally, and shrugged.

"Your people aren't here?"

Michael shrugged again. "These people say nobody from the trailers is missing. I guess my folks got out and left before the worst of it."

"They must wonder where you are. They must be so scared for you."

"I doubt it."

"You want to look for them?"

"Where?" Michael seemed almost indifferent. With a rush, Bud realized his own family cared about each other. "I'd better phone Mrs. Hechler's house and tell her to let my folks know."

"I did that already," Michael said. "I hope that's okay with you."

"Thanks, thanks, Mike. Say, where are the people from the trailers being taken?" He wanted to keep talking and to keep Michael near him, so that he would not think about his arm.

Or about his father's reaction to the loss of the boat.

"Everybody has been taken to farmhouses. Some people will even sleep in barns tonight, I hear."

"Farms? I thought people would be taken to the church." The soup burned Bud's tongue. It had no taste except hot. His arm was a scalding heat under the blanket. "Are there lists of who went where?"

Michael shook his head and sat down beside Bud. "It's not the same as your search for the old man by the stream. I am sure my folks are okay; they'll be sure I'm okay. That's how we are. None of us cares very much. I lived a lot with my older brother, only last winter he married and moved to Dallas. It's different with your family; that's why I phoned them."

Bud finished the broth. He asked the red-bearded man, "What were all of you doing down there by the river just in time to help us?"

The man had a nice slow grin. "We've been pulling

people out of the trailer park for hours. What with the swollen stream that comes into the river there, and the river itself gone crazy, the water had sliced right across the road to the park and turned the place into an island. You never saw such a bunch of terrified people. Yesterday we couldn't persuade them to leave that trailer court. Today all they wanted was out and their road was gone. The river kept right on rising and when we got down there, some trailers were floating. So what the devil were you two doing out in a boat?"

A man in shirtsleeves said, "Let's see that arm," and his touch caused a flash of pain. Bud kept his eyes on Michael. When he could speak, he said to the red-haired man, "Michael and I were going to go up the creek to look for an old man. Oh!" and he shut his mouth against the pain.

"That's not too bad a break," the doctor said. "You will have to get down to the hospital and have it x-rayed."

"An old man?" Red Beard prompted.

"He's an old man who lives in a cabin up the creek a ways."

"Friend of yours?"

"Yeah. His name is Coleman. He knows so much and he taught me a whole lot about fishing and trapping and living out in the woods. He and I caught muskrat and possum and raccoon. I'm going to get a mink. He's a great person. I guess the best person I know. He . . ."

Bud slowed down and watched the eyes above the red beard. "No."

"I'm sorry. I was the one that took the body up to police headquarters yesterday. I really am sorry. I am." He stayed with Bud for a few minutes. Then he stood. "I'll get you more soup."

Bud and Michael sat silently together. For Bud the world was an ugly empty place. He would get out of bed tomorrow and there would be no Coleman to teach him how to fly-cast; no one in the cabin on the shale beach; no bringing his catches from traps to Coleman; no sharing the quiet creek, its sounds of waterfall and birds, its secret animal life. He would get out of bed tomorrow morning and the next and the next, and what would be the point in getting up? To do the things people expected him to do? To brush his teeth and go to school and do chores and eat meals and go to bed, and the canoe would be out in the shed and he wasn't going to go out in the canoe. He would just go on, with the sun coming up and the sun setting, and what use would it all be?

After a while, Michael said, "I sure would like to catch a mink sometime. Could you teach me how?"

At that moment, Bud felt too sick for it to help. But he knew what Michael meant, knew that later it was going to help. A lot.

Bud's father arrived with dry clothes, including an old coat of his own. Bud dressed, his father's hand helping, a bit awkwardly but with gentleness. They left his shirt sleeve empty and his father's left coat sleeve empty, and a stiff white sling was put on by a nurse.

"Michael," Bud said, "you come to my house. You stay there tonight."

"Thanks. I can pick up a ride over there, later. Good luck with the arm."

"Is it okay?" Bud asked his father when they were in the car.

"About Michael? We have a full house, but you can always invite Michael."

"Who is the house full of? Hechlers?"

"The church has thirty inches of water on its floor," Mac said. "The foundation is cracked and caving in. So all the people there had to be moved out. All the people from the trailer park had to be put somewhere. We took a family with three children and a cage of mice, to stay in our house. You should have seen your mother when those mice arrived!"

They drove to the hospital in Hartford, with detours around washed-out roads and over bumpy places where mud and rocks had flowed across roads. Bud would wince and his father would look sorry, at every bump. They didn't talk much. The thought of Coleman came in and out of Bud's mind. It was there and the pain in his arm was almost welcome — and it would drift away, the way pain subsides, and Bud would be happy in the new warmth of his father's affection. During the last two days, Mac had been treating Bud more like a man, Bud thought. Now, with the broken arm, he was gentle. When had Mac Taylor ever spoken to Bud Taylor in the tone of that "you can always invite Michael"? Bud looked sideways and saw the man beside him, thin, tense, very tired. Maybe the tone had been there in the past, at times, and Bud had not heard it.

"I'd like to go along again, next time you fly to Detroit," Bud said. He could find out about its being fun.

His father sighed and shifted his back against the car seat as if his shoulders ached. "Good; I thought maybe you didn't like going with me." Then he talked about the people who couldn't be bothered boiling their water, wouldn't believe him when Mac said the water from the faucets was unsafe now. He told Bud he had spent most of the day driving out over the countryside, trying to find home owners willing to take in homeless people. "Most don't want the trouble," he said.

"You know so much about weather," Bud said. "I was glad you'd told me about it when I was in the eye of the storm. That was great."

Mac smiled. "Great, was it?"

They talked about the storm, then, as the car took them through country roads to city streets, toward the hospital. Mac said the river had crested and was staying at crest. "We'll have four more days before that water subsides and the river is back in its former banks."

"It will be all over in four days?"

"Months, it will take months." Bud heard the weariness in his father's voice as he said, "Clean-up, repairs, rebuilding."

"I'll help. My arm will heal and I can do a lot."

"I know," his father said. "You and I will have to rebuild our dock. And buy a new boat. This one will be yours . . . your own motorboat. You'll get more use from it than I ever did."

Bud's arm was hot pain, but he felt good.

After three hours at the hospital, he went home with a cast on his arm and his father's coat around his shoulders, home through dark roads to have dinner with his family and Michael.

AUTHORS' NOTE ✠ The events in this story are fictional, but the flood itself is based on the record of several floods in the Connecticut River Valley. As described here, the flood is a record-breaker, resulting directly from a specific combination of circumstances. In spite of many flood-controlling improvements which the Army Corps of Engineers has built along the river, these circumstances could recur, bringing another big flood.

The winter had been very cold with heavier than normal snow build-up and little or no thawing in January or February. Heavy ice formed in the streams and rivers running into the Connecticut, and at the beginning of March was a foot thick at Hartford. Then the temperature turned unseasonably warm and remained so. Thawing of snow and ice started an increase in run-off all up the valley and the river rose by three feet. Rain, moving in from the southwest, dropped a couple of inches over the country as it continued up the valley toward Canada. The ground, being slow to thaw, could not absorb this rain and melting snow, so most of it, draining from the mountains of Massachusetts, Vermont, and New Hampshire, ran into the Connecticut River. The river rose to a depth of twenty feet at Hartford.

Then a new and much more severe rainstorm moved up the Atlantic coast, joined with another storm coming from the west, and produced a vast area of very low barometric pressure and heavy rain centered near the coast of Connecticut. Because this storm was blocked by a high pressure area located to the north over the Gulf of St. Lawrence, its movement was slowed and the downpour continued to drench this area for two days, carrying the river above flood stage and through a record-breaking rise of another eight feet in the next twenty-four hours.

By then all emergency reservoirs were filled. Ten miles downriver from Hartford, little work had been done with diking and flood reservoirs to control the water. As a result, in the area near the site of this story, the flood spread out, inundating up to as much as a mile from the river channel in some places.

Devastation reached into the low ground, displacing many people, destroying farms, washing out bridges and roads, disrupting sewage systems, short-circuiting electric power, and seriously curtailing rescue and salvage operations. Barns and farm equipment disappeared, houses were undermined, toppled, and swept away to form river-clogging dams downstream, which would hold back the flow and delay the river's settling back within its banks.

It was another week before the river receded enough so that the laborious job of clean-up and damage assessment could be started.

Damages on the Farmington River, which flows into the Connecticut above Hartford, provide an example of the almost unbelievable power of water. The Mad River enters the Farmington at Winsted, Connecticut. It went on a rampage. It tore out a mile of Winsted's main street, cutting a new channel to a depth of ten to fifteen feet. Some sixty buildings were destroyed, including a three-and-one-half story hotel which was undermined and washed away, and five bridges completely destroyed.

Along the section of the river where the Taylors lived, families driven from their homes would see many weeks — even months — go by before clean-up, repairs, and reconstruction restored their flood-stricken area.